*"I'm going to move to New York!"* I announced grandly.

*I might as well have said I was planning to fly to the moon with no supply of oxygen.*

*"Oh, no, you're not!"* Daniel said.

*"You can't!"* Jamie said. *An expression of shock froze her face.*

*"If my father lets me, I will. If he refuses to finance me, I'll earn enough money for my plane ticket."*

*"But why?"* Jamie asked.

*"You know why. I want to be an actress."*

*"You can be one here,"* Daniel pointed out.

*"It's not the same here."*

*"Acting is acting,"* he insisted. *"You can be an actress anywhere."*

*"The opportunities are* there!*"* I shouted. *Why did they have to be so dense?*

Dear Readers:

Thank you for your unflagging interest in First Love From Silhouette. Your many helpful letters have shown us that you have appreciated growing and stretching with us, and that you demand more from your reading than happy endings and conventional love stories. In the months to come we will make sure that our stories go on providing the variety you have come to expect from us. We think you will enjoy our unusual plot twists and unpredictable characters who will surprise and delight you without straying too far from the concerns that are very much part of all our daily lives.

We hope you will continue to share with us your ideas about how to keep our books your very First Loves. We depend on you to keep us on our toes!

Nancy Jackson
Senior Editor
FIRST LOVE FROM SILHOUETTE

# A WISH
# TOO SOON
## Lainey Campbell

*First Love from Silhouette*
Published by Silhouette Books New York
**America's Publisher of Contemporary Romance**

SILHOUETTE BOOKS
300 E. 42nd St., New York, N.Y. 10017

Copyright © 1986 by Elaine Campbell Smith

All rights reserved, including the right to reproduce
this book or portions thereof in any form whatsoever.
For information address Silhouette Books,
300 E. 42nd St., New York, N.Y. 10017

ISBN: 0-373-06206-0

First Silhouette Books printing October 1986

All the characters in this book are fictitious. Any
resemblance to actual persons, living or dead, is purely
coincidental.

SILHOUETTE, FIRST LOVE FROM SILHOUETTE and
colophon are registered trademarks of the publisher.

America's Publisher of Contemporary Romance

Printed in the U.S.A.

RL 5.4, IL age 11 and up

**LAINEY CAMPBELL** recently moved from Jacksonville, Florida, to a small fishing village on the Gulf coast where she is renovating a cottage by the sea. Before turning to writing fiction, she owned a dance studio where she taught ballet and tap dancing, as well as tumbling, break-dancing and aerobics. She has also been involved with the theater. She attended summer stock, studied drama at Yale, and earned her degree in Theater Arts from Florida State University. For pleasure, Ms. Campbell plays the violin, listens to classical music, rides her moped, sits on the sandy coast and watches sea birds, and reads, reads, reads.

# Chapter One

The first thing that struck me when I got back home and went into my bedroom was how huge it was. Before, I'd never thought it was big, but compared to the tiny apartment Mom had in New York and the even tinier area I was allotted while I was visiting her, my room was gigantic. I felt on the fringes of agoraphobia—I was afraid of the wide open spaces. And this was just *my* room, the rest of the house was bigger. And no one lived in it but Dad and me.

Soon just Dad would, if I had my way.

"Are you glad to be home, Teresa?" he asked, coming in the door behind me.

"Uh, Dad—" I started, then stopped, thinking maybe it wouldn't be wise to tell him right away that I wanted to go back to New York City and live with Mom. I knew how he felt about me staying in Jacksonville with him while I finished high school. He and Mom had talked it over before she left and they had decided, without once asking me what I wanted, that I would live with him and visit Mom during the summers and sometimes at Christmas.

No, the first words out of my mouth after I walked in the house shouldn't be that I wanted to leave it again. I decided to give him a couple of days, or at least an hour or two, and *then* hit him with my idea.

With a grunt, he heaved my overstuffed suitcases onto the bed. "What did you do?" he asked, faking exhaustion. "Buy out the Village?"

"SoHo, too," I said and grinned at him. "They had some terrific sales. Mom and I went shopping almost every day the last couple of weeks I was there."

He looked concerned. "You gave her time to paint, didn't you?"

"Oh, sure. We didn't go anywhere until she had finished work for the day."

"That's good."

"She's really talented."

"I know," he said, frowning slightly, and I thought maybe I ought to avoid the subject of Mother's art for a while, too. He wasn't happy about her being away from him.

My parents aren't divorced, they're just living apart so Mom can concentrate on her art. For years and years and years, she worked to help Dad get started in the real estate business, and after he set up his office she was his secretary. Plus she took care of me. After he was firmly established and I was old enough to take care of myself, she said she wanted to devote some time to her art and go where she would have the most advantages. Dad had to agree. He's an okay guy. So last year she moved to New York into a room in Greenwich Village, but before long she found an apartment she could afford. It was a small one, for sure. I can testify to that. And now she's set to have some of her work shown in a gallery. She really is good. Someday she'll be as well-known as Picasso or Grandma Moses. I'd be willing to bet on that.

I want to be in the arts, too, but not in painting, you'd better believe. I've never even been able to draw a straight line, and any time I tried anything more complicated than that, no one knew what it was, so I gave up the thought of being a painter when I was nine years old. Maybe ten. What I want to be is an actress. This summer I learned that New York City is absolutely the best place to be if that's what you want. And I want it more than I've ever wanted anything.

"Dad," I said, again ready to break my news prematurely, but the phone rang and kept me from it.

"That's probably Jamie," he said.

Jamie is my best friend; I've known her since we were in first grade. She's short and cute and bouncy and smart, and nothing at all like tall, lean, lanky me. We are almost total opposites, but the only bad thing about our friendship is we can't trade clothes. She probably wouldn't, anyway. We don't exactly have the same taste.

"I'll get it," I said, and to save time I jumped on the bed and scrambled toward the phone on the opposite side.

Dad said, "She called twice before I left for the airport."

"You should have told her when my plane was due."

"I did tell her, but it didn't make any difference. I don't think the girl has a watch."

I laughed and said, "She doesn't," and grabbed the receiver. "Jamie!" I didn't bother to say hello; just like Dad, I knew who it would be.

"Do I sound like Jamie?" Daniel asked in exaggerated deep tones.

"Dan!" I was just as glad to hear him as I would have been to hear Jamie. Daniel and I have known each other almost forever. A long time ago before Dad started buying one place after another and fixing them up and selling them—that was part of the real estate business, he assured Mom and me each time we had to move—I lived next door to Daniel and we played together and have been friends ever since. After I got in high school we began to date now and then. Nothing serious. He is a year ahead of me and will be a senior when we go back to school next Monday. Without a doubt, he is one of the best-looking boys ever to grace those hallowed corridors, and a lot of girls are mad at me because they say I have an inside track with him and don't appreciate it. What's to appreciate? We're friends.

"Did you have a good time in New York?" Dan asked.

"It was fantastic. Wait till I tell you."

"I'm listening. Tell me."

"I can't right now." Dad was leaving the room but he was still close enough to hear me, and what I wanted to tell Daniel most was that I planned to go live with Mom. "I'll tell you when I see you."

"How about seeing me now?" he said.

"I'm waiting for a call from Jamie. Dad said she's called two times already."

"Will you see me after you talk to her?"

His eagerness puzzled me. Sure, he'd written me and even phoned me a couple of times while I was in New

York, but I'd never known him to be in such a hurry. "I guess so," I said.

"Then talk to her."

"What?"

"*Talk* to her."

I looked at the receiver as if the inanimate object had become unreasonable, then I said, "How can I talk to her when you have the line tied up?"

"Give it a shot," he said.

"Daniel, you're crazy."

"I may be crazy but I'm sure not Daniel," Jamie said.

For a moment I thought I might be the one who was crazy, then I realized. "You're at Daniel's house."

"Gee," she said innocently. "Am I?"

Daniel lived miles from Jamie and as far as I knew she had never visited him. "What are you doing there?"

She chuckled, and the sound was filled with mischief. "I thought I'd pick him up then pick you up and we'd go somewhere and get a pizza. You haven't eaten dinner, have you?"

"What do you mean pick me up?"

"I mean pick you up. In the car."

"The car?"

"Mom's car. She let me use it."

"She let you use her car? She wouldn't. You don't have a driver's license."

"Oh, yes I do."

"No you don't!"

"Yes I do." Again she laughed. "You don't think I sat around doing nothing while you were in New York, do you? I got my license."

That news astonished me. "You *didn't*!"

"I did."

"You rat!" For two years we'd planned on getting our licenses together, and she'd done it alone while my back was turned. "You're a traitor!"

"Does that mean you don't want me to pick you up?"

"No. It means I'll never forgive you."

"It does not," she said. "You're exaggerating again. Anyway, if you'd stayed in Florida, you could have gotten your license when I got mine."

"But, Jamie," I wailed, "you knew I'd be back."

"I couldn't wait for you to get back. Mom needed me to chauffeur Chucky to his ball games this summer."

"Hum," I said.

"I had no choice."

"Hum," I repeated.

She giggled—she knew I was going to forgive her— and said, "Is forever over yet?"

"I don't know. I'm not sure." Then I remembered that no one needs a driver's license in New York City because only rich or insane people have cars there; everyone else rides buses or subways or takes taxis. I might never need to get a license. "I guess so," I said.

"Good. Then I'll be by to pick you up in five minutes."

"I'll be with her," Daniel yelled in the background, "even though I'll be taking my life in my hands."

"I won't kill him," Jamie said and hung up before I had a chance to tell her I hadn't unpacked and was sticky from the trip and hadn't asked Dad if I could go so soon after getting home. I'd scarcely said hello to him.

"Dad!" I yelled out the door. "Jamie and Dan want me to go for pizza. Is that okay?" I stripped off my shirt and tried to dump a suitcase at the same time. Since I'd spent all that money and all that time shopping, one thing for sure I wanted to do was wear something new. "Is that okay?"

I thought he said okay, but by the time he answered I had the shower on and was under the spray. No one had ever bathed faster. I was out in one minute flat, sifting through the clothes on the bed for just the right outfit. I found it. It was so chic and modern and ultra that it was almost bizarre. I loved it. And to go with it I put on possibly the ugliest pair of shoes ever designed and executed by man. I loved them, too.

When I went into the living room to check and be sure Dad had said I could go, he put down his paper and looked at me. He stared at me. "Good grief," he said.

"Like it?" I did a model's turn, posing.

He seemed thunderstruck. "Your mother let you buy that?"

"Sure. Everyone in the city wears this sort of thing. Mom has an outfit almost identical."

"Shoes, too?" he asked, looking appalled.

"They're the most comfortable things I've ever had on."

"They'd have to be. They need a redeeming quality."

"Dad!" I said, feeling my style was being disparaged.

He grinned. "You look wonderful. I don't know anyone else who could carry those clothes the way you do." He paused. "Except maybe your mother."

"It's our height," I said. "And thinness."

"And elegance," he added. "You are both elegant women."

That comment made me rush to give him a hug. "Thanks, Dad." As I pulled away I felt a little guilty for wanting to go live with Mom because then he would have no one. Just to get it over, I almost blurted out again what I wanted to do, but he had what could have been a trace of tears in his eyes so I kept my mouth shut. A rare occurrence for me, and I'd done it three times already today.

"You'd better go," he said, sounding kind of misty. "Your friends are here."

How he knew that, I don't know, because I'd heard nothing, but the moment he stopped speaking a knock came at the door. I took a half step toward it, then stopped; Dad seemed too sad.

"Mom's okay," I said. "She's doing fine."

"I know she is. I know she is."

"After she gets established as an artist maybe she'll come home."

He lifted a shoulder. "Maybe so."

"She'll be able to paint anywhere then, and ship her work," I said. "As good as she is, and the way she's going, that time can't be far off." I immediately began to worry for fear she would come home before I had a chance to move in with her. I hoped that wouldn't happen.

That thought made me feel guiltier than ever and I sidled toward the door. "I'd better go."

As if to emphasize my intention, the knock vibrated anew and Daniel shouted, "Terry, come on!"

"Coming!" I shouted back and glanced at Dad.

"Go on," he said.

Daniel and Jamie were as impressed—or is the right word *stunned*—by my clothes as Dad had been, and everyone, I mean everyone, in the pizza parlor turned to look at us when we walked in there a few minutes later. Part of the reason for that could have been the stair-step picture we made: Jamie is five feet nothing inches, I'm five feet seven inches and Daniel stands an even six feet tall. Bam, bam, bam we went in the door with me in the middle, and everyone shut up and stared.

Jamie leaned toward me. "Having people look at you is good if you want to act," she whispered.

"They're looking at all of us."

"Think again," she said. "This always happens when you go into a room. But I guess you wouldn't dress the way you do if you didn't want to be looked at."

"There's nothing wrong with the way I'm dressed."

"I should say not," Daniel murmured. "You're sensational."

I grinned at him. "Thank you."

"Okay, you two," Jamie said, "Knock off the mush and let's get a table."

We slid into a booth, Jamie on one side and me then Dan on the other. "What'll we have?" he asked, sitting last.

"Large," Jamie said. "With everything."

"No anchovies," I told her. "I can't stand anchovies."

"Since when? You used to love anchovies."

"That was before I found you could buy them by the can." My mouth puckered and watered in remembrance. "I bought some. And ate them—" I paused "—all."

"One can?"

I shook my head. "Four."

"Four cans of anchovies?" She was astounded.

"At one sitting?" Daniel asked.

I shrugged. "So I'm an addictive personality."

"You're *crazy*," Jamie said. "No one in their right mind could eat four cans of those salty things at one sitting."

"I did," I said. "Easy. So no anchovies, please."

Daniel chuckled. "No anchovies," he told the waitress, "but everything else." He glanced at me. "Unless you have something more to tell."

"No. That's my only secret."

"Then large," he said, and the waitress left.

I said, "Except for one thing."

They both looked at me.

For a deliberately suspenseful moment I looked back at them, then I blurted, "I'm going to move to New York City." It was a relief to get to tell someone. I hadn't made up my mind what I was going to do until I was on the plane heading home or I wouldn't have been here now. I would have been with Beaker and some of the kids in the Village.

I might as well have said I was planning to fly to the moon with no oxygen supply.

"No you're not," Daniel said.

Jamie looked as though someone had pushed her into a pool of icy water. An expression of shock froze her face. "You can't."

"I'm going to try," I said.

They both started talking at once then, telling me how busy and dirty the city was, how I didn't know anyone who lived there other than my mother, how cold it was in the winter. Jamie threw in a few derogatory comments about the Yankees—and she was *not* talking about the baseball team. The things she said would make you think the war between the states was still going on and I would be hanged as a spy if I went north.

They ended with Dan again ordering me not to go and Jamie repeating, "You can't."

"If my father lets me, I will," I said. "Even if he won't," I added, making up my mind to earn enough money to buy a ticket if he wouldn't finance me.

"But why?" Jamie asked.

"You know the answer to that. I want to be an actress."

Daniel said, "You can do that here."

"It isn't the same here. You know it isn't the same."

"Acting is acting," he said. "You can be an actress anywhere."

"The opportunities are *there*."

"So's the competition," said Jamie.

At that moment, the pizza parlor door opened and a girl came in. I'm not certain but I think some other kids were with her. I didn't notice. She was gorgeous with dark, ebony dark, and glossy hair and the most riveting face I had ever seen. And her clothes were as eye-catching as mine. Maybe even more so.

I would swear not a word was spoken for the length of time it took her to cross to a table. Now I knew what went on in people's minds when I came into a room and conversation stopped. Not much. Just marveling disbelief that gradually dissipated so talk could resume. I leaned over and whispered to Jamie (it seemed irreverent to speak above a whisper), "Who's that?"

She shrugged, not taking her gaze off the dazzling new addition. I shook her and she looked at me. "Who's that?" I repeated.

"I don't know," she said and went back to looking at the girl.

"That girl does for brunette hair what you do for blond, Terry," Daniel said. He was still staring at her.

I punched him on the shoulder. "Ouch! That's a first! You're finally living up to the promise of your green eyes."

"Oh, no," I said. "I'm not jealous."

He quirked his eyebrow. "No?"

"No."

"That one wants to be an actress, too," Jamie commented.

I took another quick glance at the ravishing female. "How do you know?"

"I can tell."

"Don't kid me."

"I'm not kidding. I *can* tell. She has the same quality you do, Teresa. A kind of take-over-the-world way about her like you. She's on stage. Or ought to be."

I looked again. "I wonder if she'd going to be in school with us."

"What does that matter?" Jamie said. "You won't be here. You're going to New York to take Broadway by storm."

"I didn't say that."

"That's what you're thinking."

"I am not. I'm thinking of being where—"

"Where the opportunities are," Daniel interrupted.

"Right. I can't think of a single reason that would make me want to stay in Jacksonville, Florida."

Both he and Jamie glared at me as if I'd said something profane, and just then the pizza was plopped steaming in front of us. Dan got up. "Here's for my share," he said and threw some dollars on the table, "I have to go." And he left without another word.

"What's with him?" I asked, bewildered.

"Don't tell me you don't know."

"Know what?"

"Oh, good grief," Jamie said. "He doesn't want you to leave Jacksonville. He's, as they say, serious about you."

"About *me*?"

"Of course about you. Who else?"

It was my turn to say "Oh, good grief."

"Well, he is."

"But he's a *friend*."

"Yeah. Who doesn't date anyone else."

"He doesn't? But he *knows* we're just friends."

"Yeah. Uh-huh." She lifted a wedge of pizza and strung the cheese into her upturned mouth; she looked like a baby bird. She bit off the tip of the slice and said around chewing, "And he *knows* if you go to New York now that's where the relationship between you two will stay."

"Well, that's too bad, because I'm *going* to New York." I made like a baby bird myself. With my mouth full, I said. "I guess it's a good thing I didn't mention Beaker to Daniel, then."

"Beaker?"

"A guy I met. He lives in Mom's apartment building." I hooked a finger over my nose to make an arc. "He has the most extravagant nose. It's like a beak. That's why he's called Beaker. He's nice. He's trying to break into the theater and said he would help me when I came up."

"If," she said.

"When," I countered.

"If," she repeated and gave me a knowing look. "You haven't asked your dad."

"When," I repeated. "I've made up my mind."

"Oh, yeah? What does your mom think about you living there? Have you asked her?"

I looked at the pizza.

"You haven't," she said.

Why did she have to know everything?

# Chapter Two

Many times I've read stories in which people wake up and don't know where they are, and in movies after the detective or spy or whatever gets knocked out or after the heroine faints they come to and say, "Where am I?" but I never really believed that sort of thing happened. It does. When I woke that first day back in my own room in good old Jax, I didn't know where I was. Nothing registered as reality; everything looked bright and clean and strange—like part of a Walt Disney movie. The pale avocado-and-navy print of the drapes, though I'd picked it out myself, seemed alien. The furniture, though I'd lived with it at least half my life, looked unfamiliar. And the walls and ceiling, though I'd painted them myself, were much too white and bare and far away.

I expected, I guess, to bang my elbow on the bookcase that was crammed next to the bed I had used in

Mom's apartment the way I had every morning I woke up there, and be closely surrounded by dark walls that were virtually covered with objets d'art—mostly Mom's. Here, I had only one painting—hers, an early one of the ocean off Jacksonville Beach, and it hung forlornly on the wall next to the closet door. The dominant colors in it were echoed by my drapes.

It wasn't until I saw the pile of clothes I hadn't gotten around to tending to last night that I knew for sure where I was. And I was not happy about it.

The moment I realized this, my feet hit the floor. As soon as I got dressed, I was going to tell my father what I wanted to do. It wasn't fair to him not to let him know, and it wasn't fair to me to have to stay here.

But when I started looking for something to wear, I got sidetracked into hanging things up and putting things away—and putting off telling him. What if he said no? Not knowing was worse than knowing the worst.

"Dad!" I yelled and ran into the hallway before I could change my mind. "Dad! I've got to talk to you."

"I'm in the kitchen," he called.

As if a thousand hounds were after me, I tore down the hall and rounded the corner to see him standing calmly beside the refrigerator. He was drinking orange juice, but he put the glass down when he saw me. "Good morning," he said.

"Morning," I replied. I didn't know if it was good yet.

He smiled. "It's great to have you home again, Teresa. You don't know how much I missed having you around. It was so quiet."

"Don't say that!"

"Don't say what?"

"That you missed me."

"Why not? I did. Is there a law that says a father can't miss his daughter when she's not around?"

"No, but—"

He waited a second. "But what?"

"Dad," I said and that was all. Sometimes I wonder about myself; I get things just right in my mind, figure out just what I'm going to do and what I'm going to say, then can't do or say it. No wonder I want to be an actress. That way someone else writes the words and someone else even tells me what to do and I don't have to make a single decision about anything.

He took another sip of orange juice. "You said you wanted to talk to me?"

"I do."

Again he waited and I watched him as though he were a cobra getting ready to spit in my eye. I knew he was going to say no. "So talk," he said.

I fingered the hem of my shorts and shifted my weight from foot to foot a dozen times at least as I tried to get courage. I cleared my throat. I fidgeted.

He drained his glass and put it aside and asked, "Would you like some juice?"

My shoulders went up in a shrug. How did I know if I wanted juice?

"I'll get you some." He turned his back to open the door to the refrigerator.

Not having to look him in the face released me from my timidity. I took a deep breath and got prepared to be assertive. But my voice wasn't in on the positive reinforcement; it came out as a squawk. "I want to live with Mom."

Calmly, he pulled out the carton and poured. "'Fraid not," he said as he handed my juice to me.

What could I do but take it? I almost dropped it. "Dad, I have to." My voice still sounded as though it needed oil, and now it wobbled as though it needed ball bearings, too. "Dad, I really do have to."

"Your mother and I want you to finish high school here, Teresa. You know that."

"But you never asked me what I wanted," I said, trying not to whine. "I want to finish school in New York. The schools there are—"

"No."

"That's where all the advantages are. That's where I can learn to be—"

"No."

"Dad, you're not *listening* to me. I want to be an actress, and I want to go—"

"I *am* listening, and I know what you want to be, but you can't go live with your mother, and that's final."

"That's not fair," I said, straightening up and squaring my shoulders. My voice finally got into the act and leveled out. "You're being unreasonable."

"I'm being a father."

"Just because you're a father doesn't mean you have to be a tyrant. I'm sixteen years old and I—"

"And when you're eighteen you can make your own decisions."

"But I've made one now. I want to go to New York. I've decided to go to New York."

He smiled.

A smile is supposed to be an indication of friendliness, right? Wrong. Not all smiles. Not the way fathers smile when they know they have all the power on their side. He could have screamed no at me a dozen times and it wouldn't have said no as effectively as that smile did.

"I've got to go to work," he said and patted my shoulder as he went past. "Good to have you home, Duchess."

No wonder he called me duchess—he was acting like royalty. Master of everything. Needless to say, I didn't tell him it was good to *be* home.

The minute he was out the door, I phoned Mom and told her what I wanted. Did you ever have déjà vu? The conversation with her was a replay of the one with Dad. I didn't even have to see the smile to know it was equally as final as Dad's had been.

My next call was to Jamie. "Parents!" I screamed when she answered.

"What about them?"

"They're impossible, that's what. They do not understand."

She laughed; we'd agreed on this subject many times. "What don't they understand now?"

"That I have to live in New York City."

"Oh," she said softly, and I remembered how last night she hadn't thought my idea was the greatest.

But I'd already opened my mouth and put my foot in, so I went on with it. "Do you have any money?"

She was quiet a moment, then said, "Some."

"You wouldn't consider lending me enough to buy a plane ticket, would you?"

"I don't have *that* much."

"A one-way ticket," I said. "When I get there, I'm never coming back."

"Then I wouldn't give it to you if I had it," she said, sounding just about as bad as my mother.

"Well, thanks a bunch," I said.

"You're very welcome."

"Jamie, you're being as impossible as a parent," I told her. "But I'm going with or without your help. Or anyone's. I'll get a job and save enough to fly up there, and then I'll turn up on Mom's doorstep. That way she won't be able to say no."

"I don't know what's gotten into you," Jamie said. "You know you can study here."

"It's not the same here. New York is—"

"You know what?" she interrupted me. "You're turning into a bore. All you've talked about since you got back is *going* back."

"It's the only place there is. You know?"

"Is that right?" she asked, sounding definitely huffy. "I think it would come as a surprise to a lot of people around here to know that they live noplace. Listen, Terry, not only are you becoming a bore, you're becoming a snob." She hung up on me.

She'd never done that before in her life, and I was so astonished I could do nothing but look at the phone.

*Was* I a bore? She hadn't said anything about our subject matter last night after Daniel left and all we had talked about was— Oh, yes. No wonder she was bored with me. I had told her everything Mom and I did, I talked about every place I'd seen, I filled her in on Beaker and his attempts to break into theater, I'd gone on and on about how I was going to do the same thing. But a snob? "I am not!" I said to the receiver when I finally remembered to hang it up.

Jamie wasn't the only friend I had, and if she wouldn't help me I knew someone who would. Daniel.

I had dialed his number before I remembered how he'd gotten up and walked out the night before after I'd said I wasn't sticking around, so when he answered, I changed my tune; I didn't ask to borrow money and I didn't say anything about going anywhere. I said, "I need to find a job."

"Oh?" Even without seeing him I could see his eyebrow go up. "What for?"

That was a perfect opening if I'd ever heard one, but I resisted. "I need money."

"You baby-sit," he said. "You get paid for that."

"But baby-sitting isn't something I can count on. It's irregular. I need something that pays regularly."

"Doing what?"

"I don't care." I didn't. I wanted to go to New York so badly that I would have dug ditches if the hours were right. "Doing anything that pays."

He chuckled. "I'm giving up my job at the supermarket when school starts. You could apply for that."

"Daniel, I'm serious. You know you would keep your job if they would let you work only after school. I'll be going to school, too, you know."

"Oooooh," he said, drawing out the word as if he really hadn't known that. "You want a *part*-time job."

"Right."

"After school?"

Sometimes he could be perverse. "That's right."

He laughed again. "Then why don't you apply to teach in a day-care center after school? Lots of little schoolkids pile in, then have to stay until their folks get off work, and sometimes the owners hire extra help to handle the overflow. If regular is what you want, regular is what you'd get. Every afternoon after school until six. That's what I'm going to be doing. I'll be teaching a course in karate starting next week."

"You will?" He hadn't told me that. But then he hadn't stayed around to tell me much of anything.

"Yeah. The pay's pretty good, too. It's above minimum wage. And I think you could get a job in one of those places. At least you could try. If you don't want that, there are always hamburger joints. The hours aren't as good at those, though, and they don't pay as much."

Pay was what I was interested in. "Tell me more about this day-care work," I said. "What kind of activity other than karate do they want?"

"Anything kids like."

"What could I teach?"

"You were pretty good in tumbling a couple of years ago," he said. "They might want that. You could ask. That's what I did."

"I'll do that," I said, thinking I would have to get my bicycle out of the garage and hit the centers near high school, thinking if I had a car my range would be wider and I could be sure of getting to work on time if I got a job, and thinking about Mom's car sitting in that same garage doing nothing but waiting for Dad to drive it now and then to keep it running. Maybe I would get a driver's license, after all. Surely Dad would sign the consent form.

"Do you want me to pick you up and drive you to a few?" Dan was saying.

I came out of my thoughts pronto. "Of course I do."

We had to visit only three before I found a woman who was interested in hiring an assistant. Luckily for me, the place was halfway between high school and a grade school that every afternoon flooded the center with kids from kindergarten, first, second and third grades. I would be able to get to work on time even if I had to walk.

"I know your father," Mrs. McQuaide, the owner-operator, said. "He sold me this place years ago." She smiled. "You were with him and you weren't much older than the children you'll be working with."

"I don't remember," I said, then wondered if I should have said that. I hoped not remembering wouldn't affect my getting the job.

"I didn't expect you to," she said, and I relaxed. "You'll have to get a physical and have the report sent to me."

"All right." I had to get one for school, anyway.

"That's regulations," she said. "And I'll need three references."

"Okay." That wouldn't be difficult. I could ask some of my teachers or some of the parents I baby-sat for.

"You will have a locker, so, if you want, you can leave your leotards and tights here."

"Okay." Following Daniel's advice, I had told her I would teach tumbling.

"We schedule the classes on a six-week basis," she went on. "I find the youngsters get bored with any activity after that length of time and it's wise to change, so you'll have that long to think of something else you can offer."

I immediately started trying to think of something. Then I thought again. If I saved my money, by the end of six weeks I would have enough to pay my way to New York. I grinned. And if I got any baby-sitting jobs I'd have a little spending money, too.

Mrs. McQuaide reminded me again to get the doctor's report and the reference letters to her as soon as possible. "I'm sure you'll work out fine," she said.

I was still grinning when I went to join Daniel. He was leaning against a tree in the front yard, looking over the fence at some little kids playing on a swing set.

"You got the job," he said when he saw me.

"It looks that way."

I don't know who was prouder of me for getting the job: me, Dad, Daniel or Jamie. When I phoned Jamie after my interview to apologize for being a bore and a snob, I carefully didn't say one word about that city up north but talked about school and clothes and boys. She forgave me. I knew she would. And we were right back where we were before.

Except she borrowed her mother's car and came by and picked me up the first day of school. I'll have to give it to her, though—she didn't rub it in as much as she could have.

To me, she looked too young to be driving, and I looked too old not to be. It's funny, when someone is smaller than you are you tend to think they're younger even if they're not. And Jamie is not. She's two months older than I am.

"I don't know why you haven't asked your dad to sign the consent form so you can get your unrestricted license," she said to me as she looked for a parking space in the crowded student lot. "I'll get Mom to let you use this car for the test if that's the hang-up."

"A car isn't the problem," I told her. "I haven't had time. I haven't been back a week yet."

"Still," she said, and I knew she considered being able to drive more important than almost anything.

She found an empty slot and darted in, slamming on the brakes just millimeters from the bumper of the car facing us.

"Maybe I *will* get my license," I said. "Riding with you is dangerous."

She laughed and got out. "Lock the door," she said.

Jamie and I had homeroom together and American history and algebra. Algebra! What good will that ever do me? When does an actress ever need to know how or why $a + a = b$? But I had to take the course before I could graduate.

At lunch, Jamie and I scrambled for, and got, our favorite table in the corner. Not two minutes later Daniel joined us. He looked tall and handsome and shiny and scrubbed as though he were going to meet someone important, but almost everyone looked that way on the first day of school. Give us a week or two and we'd be our own scruffy selves, having learned once again, as we had to learn anew each year, that neatness goes only so far in pleasing a teacher—and then mainly if it's on paper.

He smiled and sat down beside me. "Want a ride to work this afternoon?" he asked.

"With you?" I asked and gave Jamie a sassy look. "Sure I do. That way I can be sure of getting there alive."

Jamie pointed her fork at me. "If you talk like that, I won't give you a ride to school anymore."

I grinned. "Oh, yes you will. You have to have someone along to warn you when a car is coming."

"Uh-oh, look who's here," Daniel said.

I looked. Nearly everyone in the lunchroom looked. The brunette we'd seen at the pizza parlor was making an entrance, and I do mean an entrance. She had on high-heeled shoes and hose and a dress that would knock your eyes out on the corner of Forty-second

Street and Broadway. She had gone a step beyond neatness right into vavoom.

"Wow!" Jamie said, and you could hear an echo of her all over the place. Not because she spoke loudly but because half the kids were saying the same thing. At least a dozen guys stood up, pulled out the chairs beside them and gestured for that girl to join them. Chivalry wasn't dead.

"Forevermore," I said, feeling drab in my modern top, fashionable pants and ugly shoes. "Is she a teacher or is she a student?"

"She's a student," Daniel said. "She's in second period chemistry with me."

I said, "But no one wears dresses to school."

"Evidently no one told her that," Jamie said. "But being a stand-out doesn't seem to bother her much."

The girl got her lunch and selected a seat and the room went back to normal—almost. People kept taking peeks in her direction. Me included. That's how I knew others did.

"What's your next class?" Daniel asked me.

"Drama," I said, and that perked me up and made me forget the new girl. You had to be a junior or a senior to sign up for that course, so this was the first time I would be taking it. "I can't wait."

"Me either," he said.

I looked at him. "You're going to take drama?" I couldn't believe it. He'd never shown the slightest interest in acting.

He nodded.

"That's terrific! You'll be great."

He squirmed in his seat. "I'm not interested in being great. I just thought I ought to learn something about the field."

"You'll be great, anyway. I can just see you playing Hamlet or Don Quixote or—"

"Hey! Hold on. I thought I might do some work backstage, building sets or stage managing or something."

"But you'd be a terrific actor," I said. "You look good, you sound good, you'd *be* good. Mrs. Daly will be thrilled to have you in her class."

"Mrs. Daly will have someone who would probably freeze if he had to stand in front of an audience."

"No you wouldn't. I've seen you in front of a group—last year, when you gave that speech about students becoming involved in Crime Stoppers, and you didn't freeze."

"That was different."

"Not very," I said and grinned at him. I knew he would get roles in the classroom skits and probably in the two major productions the school gives each year. "You'll see."

"And soon," Jamie said as the bell rang.

The three of us hung together as we went to the lockers, but there we had to separate because everyone else in school was at the lockers, too, and ours were spaced about as far apart as was possible and still be in the same corridor. "See you later, Jamie," I said.

"See you in a few minutes," Daniel said to me. "We'll walk to class together."

"Okay." I pushed my way through the crowd to get to my locker, which was at at the far end. On the way I bumped into the new girl. You know which one I mean. There might have been other new girls in school that year, but this one was evident.

"Pardon me," she said, as if she were the one who had done the bumping.

"My fault," I said and went on past, but I glanced back to look at her. Who wouldn't? And she was looking back at me. I couldn't tell you which one of us quit looking quickest, but I almost broke my neck getting my head turned around again. She was so stunning that everyone looked at her, and I didn't want to give her the satisfaction of knowing I was just one of everyone. Still, while I was fiddling with my combination, I tried to sneak another look at her through the press of bodies. I didn't succeed; all I saw was clean new shirts, clean new pants and clean combed hair on clean first-day students.

But so help me, when Daniel came to fetch me I was still trying to catch a glimpse of her through the now-thinning crowd. She was gone.

Within minutes I knew where she'd gone; she was sitting front and center in Mrs. Daly's classroom, which wasn't a classroom per se but had a slanted floor with a bunch of seats facing a little stage. When I saw the girl, it was all I could do to stifle a groan. Jamie had been right—she did want to be an actress.

"Wouldn't you know," I whispered to Daniel.

"Know what?"

I tipped my head toward the first row.

"*So* what?" he asked.

Sometimes the male of the species can be dense. "That girl."

"What about that girl?"

"She's gorgeous," I said. Anyone could see that, so I might as well say it. "She has presence," I admitted, though I didn't want to, but it was obvious by the turned heads she caused. "She probably has talent," I muttered, worrying that with her around I might never get a decent acting part. "And she's in this class," I finished glumly.

"So are a lot of other people," Daniel said.

He was right—the room was getting packed—drama class always had plenty of takers—and we had to rush to get seats beside each other. They were way in the back.

"Don't fret," Daniel said and took my hand and squeezed. "You're gorgeous and talented, too."

I didn't feel it.

Mrs. Daly came in and climbed onto the stage, and the chatter in the room stopped. She had presence, too. "Good afternoon," she said. "Has anyone taken this class before?"

A few hands went up.

"Then you're in the wrong place unless you've opted to take the course again without credit. Is anyone here by mistake?"

The hands went down.

"All right, then. Today I won't call roll. Today each of you will take the stage and tell your name and a little about yourself. We'll begin with those on the last row. Line up by the steps, so after one person is finished we won't have a long delay before the next one goes on."

Those of us in the back went toward the front and somehow, miraculously, I became first in line. I'm sure that's because everyone gets at least a little stage fright when they have to face an audience and the others shuffled me forward. I get stage fright, too, and this was no exception; my stomach filled with butterflies and my palms got wet.

"Go get 'em, tiger," Dan whispered.

I glanced at him. "Want to go first?"

He shook his head and gave me a nudge to the stairs.

On the way up, I tried to think of what role to play, what character to be. I couldn't be myself—that was unthinkable; I wouldn't be able to say one word if I had to be myself.

"Hi," I said after I reached center stage. I tucked my hair behind my ears. Alice in Wonderland? "I'm Teresa Carson and I was born right here in Jacksonville." My hands went to my hips and I spaced my feet apart, standing strong. Long John Silver, for heaven's sake? "I'm a junior this year, and I want to be an actress." I squinted at the faces that were staring at me, but I couldn't think of one other thing to say except maybe avast ye landlubbers. "That's it," I concluded and tried to keep from limping on my peg leg as I went off stage on the other side.

Dan was next and he did better than I did, and he didn't even want to act. He said he was Daniel Boone and that he lived in Tennessee and didn't know what he was doing here because he was a bear killer. After the kids quit giggling he told them the truth, which was a whole lot like what I'd said, but he was a senior and his last name was Hanbury and he was going to go into computer science.

"How could you do that?" I asked him after we got back to our seats. "Say you were Daniel Boone?"

He shrugged. "I thought someone ought to break the ice."

He'd done that, all right; from then on almost everyone had something cute to say; some even merited applause. And then the first row lined up and that girl was last. She took the stage with the authority of the Queen of England going behind a podium. "My name is Regan Relaford." Wouldn't you know even her name would be gorgeous? "Like Teresa, the first person on this stage today—'' hearing my name made my ears perk up more than they were already perked ''—I want to be an actress.'' She paused. ''I *will* be an actress. My father is in the navy and was transferred, so I'm new to Jacksonville. I did live in New York City where I worked with a terrific theater group, but I know I'm going to enjoy studying here more.'' How could she say that? She smiled as if she had heard my unuttered question. ''Believe it or not, there are more opportunities in this town,'' she finished.

The girl might be beautiful, but she was also crazy.

# Chapter Three

School hadn't been in session long before I knew I was in trouble. Not with my job—that was going along just fine. The children loved me and I loved the children; I had all of them doing front roll-overs, most of them doing back roll-overs, a few of them doing round-offs, and one agile girl could do a walk-over. And I knew before the six weeks were finished I'd have each kid doing a trick he or she had never done before even if that were nothing more than standing on his or her head. Mrs. McQuaide liked me, too. She was already asking what I planned to offer as the next activity.

No, my job gave me no problems. The trouble was in school. More specifically, in drama class. Regan Relaford was getting all the attention. From everyone. At least that was the way it seemed to me.

In that class the first week of school—for some ridiculous reason held during the last dog days of August when no one ought to have to go outside for any reason—we got familiar with the stage, learning up stage and down stage and upper right stage and stuff like that. And then we practiced the basics on how to move, and Mrs. Daly had Regan teaching as much as she was. If Mrs. Daly wanted someone to demonstrate how to rise from a chair without looking awkward, she asked Regan to show us how it was done; and Regan always did it right. She always walked away from the chair right, too. She never failed to start off on the up-stage foot. Everyone else tripped at least once.

"Regan is good," Daniel whispered to me once after she had made a graceful entrance, then crossed the stage in a smooth arc and never once turned her back on the audience.

"That's because she's studied in New York."

"That's because she's studied."

I glared at him and he glared back, and I would have hit him but it was my time to make an entrance and go across the stage. I moved just as easily and professionally as Regan had. Or so I thought.

During the second week, each student had to memorize and present a monologue or a poem. It was personal choice. Most of us gave short recitations maybe a half-page long, but not Regan. Hers had to have been ninety-eight pages at least, and she didn't mess up once or forget a single word. Also, she wore an outfit that enhanced her act. I could have killed her. The rest of us were in typical school clothes, which meant mostly jeans and tops, and if you can imagine someone in faded jeans and a white T-shirt, which in bright red block letters says It Isn't My Fault and in smaller cursive writing is signed San Andreas, quoting: " 'But soft! What light through yonder window breaks?' " then you have a general idea how much anyone else thought of matching clothes to speech. Daniel did that Romeo speech and I did "Dover Beach" by Matthew Arnold, and I must admit I wasn't any more appropriately costumed for my time on stage than he was. I decided that next time I would be, though.

Of course during Regan's entire one-man show, Mrs. Daly smiled. And after everyone stopped clapping—naturally we did that; Regan *was* good—she suggested that the rest of us emulate Miss Relaford and dress the part the next time we were assigned solos. So much for making my mind up on that for myself; next time everyone would be dressed appropriately.

At lunch the next day, I said to Jamie, "You ought to be glad you aren't in drama class."

"I *am* glad," she said. "I don't like acting."

"Not because of that. Because of Regan. Honestly!"

"What did she do?"

"What didn't she do? She does everything. And everything exactly the way it should be done, according to Mrs. Daly." I sighed. "I don't think the girl is capable of doing anything wrong."

"So? You don't do anything wrong, either, do you?"

I had to consider that. At one time I would have agreed with Jamie and said right off I didn't, but now I wasn't so sure. "Well—" I hedged.

"Well, do you?"

"Let's put it this way, I don't do anything as right as Regan does." I tried to stop there, but I couldn't. I said, "And it's driving me crazy. It's not fair. She's had all the luck. She got to study in—"

Daniel came then and saved me from boring Jamie again, but other than that he wasn't any help. "Regan really showed us all up yesterday, didn't she?" he said.

I gave him a look that would melt wax, but unfortunately he wasn't a Madame Tussaud mannequin. "I had just mentioned that," I said.

"She sure is talented."

"I am going to kill her," I said suddenly. I meant every word. "I really think I will."

"What did she do to you?" Daniel asked, surprised at my vehemence.

"And if I don't kill her, I'll maim her or something and put her out of commission for a long time."

"Teresa, you're talking crazy," Jamie said.

"I *am* crazy. I told you that girl was driving me that way." I calmed down a bit. "But I don't know what to do if I don't kill her."

"You could try getting along with her," Daniel suggested.

"Hah! Mrs. Daly doesn't pay any attention to anyone but Regan—"

"Good grief," he said. "That's not true."

"And I don't know how I'm going to learn anything with her around."

"It's only the second week of school," Jamie said. "Give yourself a chance."

"Give Mrs. Daly a chance," Daniel said.

And Jamie ended up with "Give Regan a chance."

"She's had more of a chance than I have," I said, feeling genuinely sorry for myself. "If I had been able to study before, especially if I had been able to study in—"

"Don't say it," Jamie cautioned.

"Well, it's true."

"You can study here," Daniel said. "That's what you ought to concentrate on, and not on how much attention Regan gets or how much more than you she knows."

"But I'll never catch up."

"Not if all you do is complain about being behind."

"That's not all I do," I said. "This is the first time I've done it."

"Aloud," Jamie put in.

I quieted her with a look. "And I do work," I added.

"Then keep it up," Daniel said. "Cooperate. Try to pick up as many pointers from Regan as you can, and quit resenting her. That won't get you anyplace."

He was right, of course, but I couldn't stop. She'd had advantages I hadn't. And I wanted them.

I would get them, too. In a couple of weeks I would get paid and be on the first step toward my goal. That thought cheered me up and I was able to eat. But afterward I had to grit my teeth so I could go to drama class and watch Regan be extraordinary. Which she was. Of course. But worse than that, she was so darned nice. Everybody liked her, with one possible exception. Me. I hadn't spoken to the girl since the day I'd bumped into her in the hall. Why should I? It was hard enough putting up with her from a distance.

I made up my mind that that evening I would talk to Dad again. Surely when he heard how Regan was taking over the only class I ever had been obsessively interested in, and that was because of the advantages she'd had by studying in New York City, then he would reconsider.

Not being totally without imagination, I planned to pick my time carefully. Ever since Mother had left, I'd done most of the cooking, if cooking was done. A lot of the time we survived on fast food, but we wouldn't tonight. The minute I got home from work I phoned Dad and told him not to pick up anything—I would take care of dinner.

And it was the best I'd made since I got home. It was all from scratch; not a canned or frozen or packaged item was put on the table that night. I even had candles.

When Dad came in, he said, "This is lovely. What's the occasion?"

"I'm trying to soften you up," I said. He'd have figured it out, anyway.

"This is definitely a good way to start," he said, grinning. "Did you pick up the mail?"

"It's on the coffee table." I should have waited until after I checked the mail before I decided to face Dad with going to New York. He didn't have a letter from Mom and that always made him unhappy. And today was no exception. When he came back into the dining room, his face looked sad.

"She'll probably write tomorrow," I said. "She can't write every day."

"I know."

"Gosh. She stays so busy."

"I know," he said again, sounding more depressed.

Sometimes I felt like the parent to my parents. It was a weird feeling having to boost their egos and give them hope for the future and try to make things seem more optimistic than they were. I didn't know if Mom ever would come back, but I never let that show; I always acted as if I knew she would. "When I was up there with her," I said, "sometimes I didn't see her for days on end. Practically. She was all the time going to art shows and gallery openings and classes and meetings. And she has to spend hours on her craft."

"I'm sorry I act this way, Duchess," Dad said. "But I miss her."

"She misses you, too."

"She's been gone a long time."

"She'll be back."

"I don't know why she can't do her work here."

"Someday maybe she will be able to."

He nodded, then gave me a little smile; it wasn't wholly real, but he was trying. "What are you softening me up for?" he asked. "You have a job now, so I know it can't be for money."

"Oh, my gosh! The roast!" I said and dashed for the kitchen. I had turned off the oven and the roast wasn't in any danger, but that hadn't been exactly the most propitious time to tell Dad what I wanted to tell him. I decided I should feed him first.

But during dinner he kept talking about Mom, about how she would have liked the food, the elegant table, the soft lights. And the fact that I had done it all on my own. I never did find the right time to broach the subject of me joining her, and Dad didn't ask again why I was softening him up. I decided it would be better to wait until I got the money for my fare together before I mentioned what I wanted to do. And then I would just tell him goodbye.

During the third week of school, Mrs. Daly brought a bunch of short plays in; we were to get together in pairs or groups and go through them and pick one we wanted to do. Everyone was to have at least one major role, and if we needed other members to fill out the cast—bit players, supernumeraries—then we were to arrange with students who were willing to double up. The skits would be self-directed, but Mrs. Daly said she would give us pointers along the way. The final performance would be due the first week of October.

"Let's do one together, okay, Daniel?" I said.

He looked at me as if surprised I'd asked. "What else?"

"I mean *just* you and me. A two-character play."

"Do you think we can find one?"

"Sure," I said. "Probably."

He quirked his eyebrows. "Then let's get busy."

Our selections were to be made by Friday, and for a few days the class looked through plays and read them. Daniel and I found what we were looking for; it was a long play but the parts were evenly balanced.

"I'm not sure I'll be able to memorize all my lines in time," Daniel said.

"Sure you will. We'll help each other."

"I'll need it."

I laughed. "So will I. Just a second, I'll go ask Mrs. Daly if we can do this one."

When I got to the front of the room, Mrs. Daly smiled at me. "Hello, Teresa."

"Hi. Daniel and I picked out a play and I want to know if it's all right."

"Oh, dear," she said. "I should have mentioned this to you sooner, Teresa. I want you and Regan to do this one-act." She picked a play up off her desk and held it toward me. "It has two characters, both female, and I'd like to see you and Regan work together."

"Regan. But Daniel and I looked through all those—"

"Going through the plays was a good exercise for you. Becoming familiar with various works is valuable. Your work wasn't wasted. I haven't told Regan, either." She gestured and called for her.

Regan stood from where she'd been bent over to talk to Dan, and that really irritated me. What did she think she was doing? She must have dashed to him the minute my back was turned. She had taken over everyone and everything else, and now she was trying to horn in on him.

"Yes, Mrs. Daly," she said.

"May I see you a moment?"

"I'll be right there." She gave Daniel the cutest wave as she left him and came toward us.

Oh, she made me burn. I wouldn't even look at her as she joined Mrs. Daly and me.

"You girls know each other, don't you?" Mrs. Daly asked.

"I know who Teresa is, of course," Regan said, "but we haven't officially met."

Officially met. Well, la de da.

"Teresa," Mrs. Daly said, "have you left us?"

I looked at her. "No."

"Is something wrong?"

I glanced at Regan, sighed and said, "No."

"Hi," she said and smiled at me. It was an absolutely dazzling smile. I'd never *seen* such straight white teeth. "I'm Regan," she said.

Big news. Everyone knew who she was. "I'm Treesa," I said. Where that name came from I'm not sure. Once in a while I'd played around with thinking of a stage name, one that would be memorable on a marquee, but that one hadn't dawned on me until this moment.

"What an unusual name," Regan said. "I thought your name was Teresa."

"No," I said loftily. "It's Treesa. You can call me Tree."

"Tree?" Mrs. Daly asked somewhat dubiously.

"That's right," I said. "Tree." I tried to match Regan's smile, but I don't know if I was successful.

"Tree," Mrs. Daly said again faintly.

"I've been watching you, Regan," I said. What an understatement. "You're good."

She said, "How generous of you to say that."

Indeed generous. Saying it had almost warped my tongue.

"Girls," Mrs. Daly said, "I want you to work together on this." She handed us each a photocopy of the play. "You can decide between you who gets which role. They are just about equal, and I think either of you could play either part, so make up your own minds."

"That's great," Regan said.

I wasn't sure it was so great; I wasn't sure I wanted to be anywhere near a stage if she was on it. Aloud I said, "But what am I going to tell Daniel?"

"I'm sure some of the other students will need his help," Mrs. Daly said. "He won't have any trouble finding a group to work with."

"Oh, he won't," Regan agreed. "I just asked him to be in my play. We needed someone else."

I said, "But I just got through telling him we were going to work together."

"But you aren't going to work with him, after all, are you, dear?" Mrs. Daly said, and smiled at me. I must admit her smile looked a little strained. "You're going to do this play with Regan." She paused meaningfully. "Aren't you? As you have been assigned."

I riffled the pages of the play I definitely was going to do, no questions asked, and said, "Yes, ma'am."

"I'd better tell the group I was working with that I'll be doing something else," Regan said. "I'll get with you in a few minutes and we can work out a rehearsal schedule. Is that okay, Tree?"

I kept riffling the pages.

"Tree?" She touched my arm.

I hadn't realized she was talking to me; I'd forgotten I'd told her to call me that. But it sounded pretty good. Better than Terry. "What?" I asked.

"Can we talk about when we're going to practice?"

"Sure." I started to tell her I worked after school and couldn't rehearse then.

"Catch you in a minute." She dashed away, leaving me with my mouth open on an unuttered word.

Mrs. Daly said, "You can learn a lot from her, Terry. I mean, Tree."

The name sounded good from her, too.

"You have promise," she went on, "and I want you to get as much out of this class as you can, so keep your eyes and ears open."

"I will," I said. I didn't want to say what I said next, but felt I should. "I'm sorry I argued about the assignment earlier, it's just that—"

"I know," she interrupted. "But you'll learn more working with Regan than you would if you worked with your boyfriend, and that is what going to school is about."

My boyfriend? I looked at her and started to argue about that, too, but figured I'd done enough arguing for one day. Especially in a class where I would be graded. "I guess I'd better tell him he'll have to find someone else to work with."

"I guess you'd better."

He'd already found someone else. A dozen someone elses, and they were all hovering around trying to talk him into joining their groups. He grinned when I approached, and said, "It's a good thing I'm doing a play with you. Everyone needs another guy in their cast."

"Pick one," I told him.

"What?"

"Pick another cast. Mrs. Daly said we couldn't do the play we chose. She gave me a different one." I sighed. "And I have to work with Regan."

His grin got bigger. "Hey, that's terrific. Everyone wants to work with her."

Do I need to tell you that made me feel swell?

The other kids crowded closer, badgering him to be in their plays, and within seconds I was staring at nothing but a bunch of backs. "Well ex*cuse* me," I said.

"Here I am, Tree," Regan said, coming up beside me. "Now we can talk about rehearsal schedule. I think we should get together every afternoon."

"I can't."

She frowned. And she looked just as pretty frowning as smiling. "Why not?" she asked.

"I work."

"Oh. That's too bad."

"I don't think so. I need the money."

"I didn't mean that." She looked flustered. "I didn't mean it was bad because you have to work, but because we can't rehearse then. It would be easier to stay after school instead of having to meet someplace."

"Why do we have to do that? We'll be working on the play during class."

"That wouldn't give us enough time. We have to practice a lot more." Her blazing smile came again.

"We can get together in the evenings, though, can't we?"

"Sure," I said. What else could I say? The girl was a steamroller.

"But first we'll have to decide who plays which part. Let's read the play tonight and you can choose the role you want. It won't matter to me one way or another."

It probably wouldn't. She could probably play any part anytime.

"See you later," she said and ducked into the crowd around Daniel. I could hear her say, "We won't need you for the part I asked you about, after all, Dan. I'm sorry. Working together would have been fun."

Dan said, "Yes, it would have, but we'll work together some other time."

You would think that with the hum of other conversations going on I wouldn't be able to hear either her or Dan, but I could. It was as if they were using loudspeakers directed right at my ears.

"I hope so," she said.

And he said, "After I decide which play I'm going to be in, maybe we could get together and you could help me. I'd like that. I'll need help."

His asking her that made me feel worse than anything I could remember. It was all I could do to keep from confronting him with how I felt before the bell rang.

I carefully avoided him and Regan that afternoon. And I walked to work. I don't know where he thought I'd vanished to, or even *if* he thought about it. For all I knew he was somewhere with Regan. Teaching her karate.

When I got to work, I was still mad. And the kids noticed. There's nothing like little kids for seeing right into how you feel. "What's wrong, Treesa?"

"Treesa, what's the matter?"

I tried to tell them nothing was wrong, but they kept at me, wanting me to smile. A really cute little five-year-old, one who never could do roll-overs straight and went off the side of the mat every time, patted me on the cheek. "Don't be sad. We don't want you to be sad, Treesa."

"I'm not sad," I told them.

"*We* like you, Treesa."

Right about then it dawned on me what they were calling me. No wonder I'd come up with that variation of my name; they'd been calling me that for weeks. I smiled.

"She's happy again," one of them said.

"Is that right, Treesa? Are you happy now?"

"Yes," I said. "I'm happy now."

And I stayed pretty happy until I got home. Dad was there, and evidently I learned something from the kids at work because I could immediately see he wasn't in a good mood. "Are you okay, Dad?" I asked.

"Yes. Yes, Teresa. I'm fine."

I saw the mail scattered around him. Obviously he hadn't heard from Mom again today.

"I brought chicken," he said. "It's in the kitchen."

"Okay," I said, and hung around a few minutes, but he didn't want to talk. I took a couple of drumsticks to my room and wrote Mom a letter asking her why she couldn't paint at home and mail her work. I told her we needed her. And we did. Both of us. At that moment I could have used a mother's shoulder to cry on.

# Chapter Four

The next morning instead of Jamie coming by to pick me up, Daniel did. He said he'd told her not to bother. And after I deigned to get in the car with him rather than walk the two miles to school, he asked, "Where did you go yesterday? I waited for you until I was almost late for work."

"I walked," I said.

"Why did you do that?"

I didn't want to explain; in the bright light of early morning, with him driving me to school, I could reflect that my action yesterday had been a little dramatic. I'd overreacted. Anyway, if I did tell him, he would probably again accuse me of being jealous. I just shrugged.

"Why did you do that?" he said again. "Why did you go off without telling me? It isn't like you to leave without letting someone know, Terry."

"Call me Tree," I said.

"Why? It's not your name."

"I like it."

"Okay, Tree. Anyway, it was rude of you to go off like that."

"Well!" I said with some heat, and forgot my reluctance to speak. "I wanted to do that play with you. I didn't want to work with Regan."

"Why not? She's the best student in the class."

I glared at him. "Tell me more."

He gave me a glance. "I didn't say she had the most talent, I said she was best. And she is. You can learn a lot if you work with her."

"Of course I can."

He touched my cheek with the backs of his fingers. "Come on, Tree, lighten up a bit. It isn't like you to be jealous. And it doesn't suit you."

"Maybe not," I said, "but she's had advantages."

"So take advantage of her advantages. You're as good as she is. Maybe better. You just need more practice."

I got it. And I needn't have worried about Dan and Regan working together; they didn't have *time* to work together. I told you Regan was a steamroller—she wanted to get together with me nearly every night to work on our play. And work is precisely *all* we did. We never went anywhere for fun, we never talked without the script as the topic of conversation and I, for one, did not particularly enjoy the time we spent rehearsing.

For one thing, she had her lines memorized at least a week before I did, but I'll have to give her credit for helping me learn mine. She was better at it and more patient than either Jamie or Daniel, though they helped me, too. Jamie wasn't a bit interested in theater and it bored her senseless to have to keep giving me cues and watching carefully to be sure I had the lines down exactly right, and I could do nothing for her in return, so I only imposed on her once. Daniel had as much trouble learning his part as I did mine, so I spent half the time I studied with him feeding him cues instead of learning my lines. Dad helped me, too, when he had time, but I could tell he would rather be reading or watching television or writing Mom. So as it turned out, Regan was my best and most dedicated coach. She had her lines down pat three days after the play was assigned, and she knew I had to know mine or the thing would bomb.

"I don't know how you memorized your part so fast," I said to her at the time. "You make me feel dumb."

"You aren't dumb," she told me. "You just haven't had as much experience learning lines as I have. I got the knack of it last year."

Yeah. *Last year when she was in New York.*

"It'll be easier after you've been at it awhile," she said.

We didn't argue much about blocking the play; usually we agreed on who should move where, but more often than not she was the one who had the best ideas, and fortunately, I recognized that. But when I had a brainstorm about movement or was sure I was right, she had the grace to at least try it out. And sometimes my ideas worked. Mostly, though, I felt like an apprentice while she was at least a journeyman, if not a master; almost every move we made and every interpretation or nuance of line came from her mind. That made me want to do something on my own. Just to see if I could.

It didn't take me long to realize I had a ready-made cast close at hand. Of course it was a young cast, but I did have to come up with a new activity for the kids in day care, and what would be better than drama?

I told Mrs. McQuaide, and she thought the plan was great. "You could do a play for Halloween," she said. "The children would love that, and so would the parents." She beamed at me. "Tree, you're a treasure."

I'd told her to call me Tree, too. I'd told everyone that except my dad.

"We'll put together a little platform for a stage and invite anyone who wants to come," she went on. "We'll have it a day or two before Halloween so it won't interfere with trick or treat." She grabbed a calendar. "How about the twenty-ninth? Can you get a play done by then?"

"Maybe a short one," I said.

"That'll be fine, Tree. A short play would be great. What we'll do is plan a costume party with the play as the centerpiece and the children can invite their parents and grandparents and friends."

Now I was faced with finding a short play that little kids could learn, and I had to do it along with homework and the play I was doing with Regan. Well, I'd asked for it, and my assignment with Regan would be over before I would have to get serious with the children, so I thought I could do it.

That was before I started looking for a play I thought the kids could do. I couldn't find one. And the days were passing swiftly; tumbling would end and I would have to begin coaching drama, but I didn't have anything to teach.

"Why don't you write the play?" Regan said to me one day when I mentioned my problem to her.

"Write a play? Me?"

"Sure. You know who you have to work with. You know you want the play to be about Halloween. You know how long it has to be. You know drama." She shrugged. "So why not? Writing a play probably wouldn't take much longer than going through the library to find one that's exactly right."

"I never thought of that."

"I'll help you, if you want."

What I wanted was to do something on my own, something Regan couldn't rule or get the credit for. I told her no thanks and went back to talking about nothing but our play for drama class—which wasn't a bad idea; we had only a few days before it was due to be performed.

Mrs. Daly had asked us from time to time if we needed or wanted help, and we had refused in concert as if we had rehearsed that, too. Even though I didn't want to do it, I had to admit that in one way Regan and I were alike; we wanted to do things on our own and we wanted to do well.

That last week before our presentation, Regan and I got together each and every night. She would be waiting at my house when I got home from work or I would go directly to hers and we would work until time to go to bed, then I would go home or she would go home. If she had been Jamie, we would have spent the nights at each other's house, but she wasn't Jamie. Dad liked her, though, as much as he liked Jamie. I told you everyone liked Regan.

The only time I had to do homework was in study hall, and the only time I had to think about the play I was going to write was while I was at work, which wasn't a bad time to think about it. I could look at the kids and try to figure out who could do what. They were so young that I knew none of them could do much, and that focused my thoughts and my aspirations. I came up with a good idea: since it was Halloween and kids always dressed up as witches and ghosts and goblins and skeletons to trick or treat, they could get costumes they would be able to use twice. Why not have a bunch of kids going trick or treating in the play? What if they, on the way, met a real witch? A little witch who was frightened of them instead of the other way around?

I was so proud of my idea that I wanted to tell someone, but I didn't because I hadn't written a word and I wasn't really sure I could.

I didn't have time to get started, either, and wouldn't for a few days; the week the class was to present the plays was upon us. The groups drew lots to see who would go first, second and so on. Fortunately for me, or unfortunately, because with every day that passed I got more and more scared of getting on that stage with Regan, we were to be next to last. That meant we had three more nights to practice and I had three more days in which to get more scared.

Daniel was in two plays, two good ones, and he did well in each of his parts. He didn't seem to be at all embarrassed or afraid or awkward. Maybe he should be the one to go into theater and not me, I thought.

"Doesn't being on stage bother you at all?" I asked him after his second appearance.

"No. Why? Should it? Does it bother you?"

"It scares me to death."

"That's probably because you want to make a profession out of acting. You want to be good and that makes you tense and gives you butterflies."

"You bet it does."

"But I'm doing this mainly just for fun, so I'm able to relax. All I want out of the class is a decent grade."

"I want that, too."

"You'll get one."

And I did. Regan and I presented our play, and after a few minutes on stage I forgot about having stage fright; my palms dried up and my stomach went back to normal and I got into my part. Neither of us goofed a single time, and after we were through the class went wild with applause and Mrs. Daly looked pleased. I was happy and so was Regan, and we actually smiled at each other.

The next week, when report cards were handed out, I had an A- for the class. Regan had an A.

Of course. *She had studied in New York.*

But I was going to do better than she did next time, or at least as well, and I knew just how to do it; I would be sure Mrs. Daly was at my Halloween play performance on the twenty-ninth if I had to kidnap her. She would have to accept the project as worth extra credit, and that ought to erase the minus, and maybe even give me A + .

By then, I was into putting words on paper and I had chosen the cast. Two parts, anyway. I was to be the big witch, the mother—I had to be, I was the only big person around—and Brenda, a darling little girl who was confident and smart, was to be the little witch. I more or less let the other kids decide what parts they wanted, and since they got to be a goblin if they wanted to be a goblin, or a ghost if that was what they wanted to be, they cooperated like crazy.

"Okay, all you witches say: 'We're witches.'" I pointed at the children who had said they wanted to dress that way.

"We're witches!" they shouted.

"You ghosts say: 'We're ghosts.' "

They did.

"Goblins say: 'We're goblins.' "

They were the loudest.

"Now everyone says: 'We come out on Halloween Night.' " They had a bit of trouble with that and had to do it several times before they remembered the line, but finally they did.

"All right," I said encouragingly after they got it, "now repeat the we're witches, we're ghosts, we're goblins part."

A few ghosts said they were witches and a few goblins said they were ghosts, but we got that straightened out shortly.

"Next, everyone says: 'We want to give you a fright!' "

I couldn't have done the line better myself. They made me jump with the last word.

"You guys are terrific," I told them. "This is going to be a wonderful play."

We rehearsed each afternoon, and they got better with every rehearsal. I was pleased with them and with myself.

As the day for the performance got closer, I started staying at the day-care center after the kids left so I could help Mrs. McQuaide decorate and rig up a stage. On the evening we shoved the platforms around, Daniel came to help us. He helped us put up lights, too. They weren't exactly stage lights, but they did serve to illuminate the stage better than the overhead fixture.

And then it was the twenty-ninth. We didn't rehearse that day; we set up folding chairs for the audience and then got into costume. Every one of those kids wanted makeup put on at the same time, and each of them wanted to be first. I had to go from one to the other, dabbing a bit here, a smidgen there, but finally they were all ready and in their masks.

The guests began to arrive. Mrs. Daly came. And Regan in an orange and black outfit—she dressed the part even if she wasn't going to be on stage. She said she wanted to see what I had done. Daniel was there, and Jamie and Dad. By the time the parents, grandparents and friends had all arrived, there was standing room only. I was getting butterflies.

But I didn't have time to dwell on my fears. Brenda, who was to be Hildy, the frightened little witch, also got a case of stage fright, and I had to soothe her.

"You'll do fine," I told her. "You know every single one of your lines, and even if you forget I'll be right there to tell you what to say. Just pretend we're practicing again."

"But we're *not* practicing," she said. "All those *peo*ple are out there."

"Sure they are. That's why we practiced. You want your mommy to see the play, don't you?"

She nodded, and her curls bounced under her peaked black witch's hat.

"Everyone else wants their mommys and daddys to see, too. No one's out there but people who like us. We'll be fine."

She leaned close to me. "Are you scared, too?" she whispered.

I smiled. "A little bit. If I forget what to say, you tell me, okay?"

She grinned. "You won't forget."

"Neither will you."

I gave her an encouraging pat and had to leave her; the other kids were like a mass of worms in a can, wriggling all over the place. With Mrs. McQuaide's help, I got them in their places so we could begin.

The stage looked like a field in autumn dress and, after another pat from me, Brenda/Hildy ran onto the stage, looking over her shoulder. "'I'm scared. I'm so scared. Where can I hide?'" She looked around. "'A haystack. The perfect place. I'll be safe there.'" She went behind it and hid.

So far, so good, I said to myself and crossed my fingers as the trick-or-treat children came on.

"'We're witches.'"

"'And ghosts.'"

"'And goblins.'"

"'We come out on Halloween Night.'"

"'We're witches.'"

"'And ghosts.'"

"'And goblins.'"

"'And we don't like the light.'"

"'We're witches.'"

"'And ghosts.'"

"'And goblins.'"

"'We want to give you a *fright*!'"

The witches cackled, the goblins shrieked, the ghosts booed and then a whooing sound was heard.

"'Quiet.'"

"'Shhh.'"

"'Listen.'"

"'What's that?'"

Everyone got quiet, and the whooing got louder.

"'Oh, no!'"

"'It's a real ghost!'"

"'I'm scared.'"

" 'Me too.' "

They clustered into two groups, hugging one another just as we'd practiced.

" 'Let's get out of here.' "

" 'Let's run!' "

And they took off the way they had come. I could hear them giggling on the other side of the stage and knew they were as proud of themselves as I was of them. But their exit was my cue, so I made my entrance. " 'Hildy,' " I called. " 'Where are you?' " I looked around. " 'Oh, dear. This is her first Halloween. She can't miss it.' "

The whooing came again, but now the sound was more like weeping. Brenda was doing a terrific job behind the haystack.

" 'Hildy,' " I called again and looked some more, and followed the sound and drew the little witch from her hiding place. " 'Hildy, what's wrong?' "

" 'I'm scared.' "

" 'Pooh! You shouldn't be scared.' "

" 'I am. I saw witches and ghosts and goblins and—' "

" 'Those weren't real witches or ghosts or goblins. You're a witch. A *real* witch. You're supposed to scare people, not the other way around.' "

" 'But *they* scared *me*. They *are* real.' "

" 'No they aren't. If I prove it will you quit being scared?' "

" 'They *are* real.' "

" 'I'll go find those children. In just a minute you'll see there's nothing to be afraid of.' " I went off stage where the other kids were waiting and brought them back with me.

"'Oh! Oh! They're going to get me,'" the little witch said, and hid her eyes behind her hands.

"'No they won't, or I'll give *them* a scare. Take off your masks,'" I said to the group. "'All of you.'"

Just as we'd planned, they refused. All together they chanted, "'We're witches and ghosts and goblins. We come out on Halloween Night. We're witches and—'"

"'Stop that! You're scaring Hildy.'"

"'Really?'"

"'Scaring a real witch?'"

They all laughed and started to remove their masks.

"'We're not real.'"

"'No. Look.'"

They went to the little witch who peeked at them. "'You *are* just children,'" she said.

"'Of course that's what we are.'"

"'We're going trick or treating.'"

"'Want to come?'"

"'We'll scare everyone.'"

"'We'll have lots of fun.'"

Hildy looked up at me. "'May I go, Mommy?'"

"'Yes. But be good. Don't scare anyone too much.'"

"'I won't.'"

The children took Hildy's hands and they went off, chanting the witches and ghosts and goblins line again. I watched them go and was so proud none of them had forgotten a line that I forgot to say "I'm so glad Hildy isn't missing her first Halloween."

No one would have heard me, anyway; the minute the kids got off stage they ran back on to chatter to me about how they had done. I wanted to give each of them a big bouquet; they'd been terrific. I was so pleased that I could have burst.

We hugged and kissed a few minutes, then they invaded the audience to hear accolades from the guests.

I got some, too. Mrs. Daly complimented me on my directing, if not my acting or writing. "The show was beautifully staged," she said. "You work well with children. They did a fine job."

"You were great," Daniel said and hugged me, knocking off my peaked hat.

Jamie caught it and put it on her own head. She looked strange in her neat blue dress, hose, high-heeled shoes and a witch's hat. "I liked your play," she said.

"I couldn't have done better myself," Regan said, which I supposed must have been a compliment.

Dad joined us and put his arm around my shoulders and kept it there. "This is my daughter," he told everyone who would listen.

# Chapter Five

Until the next Monday I felt great, full of success and accomplishment and pride. But then I was knocked back into my place, you'd better believe, and my place was one step behind Regan Relaford.

Each year our school gives two major productions, one before Christmas, and one in the spring. Mrs. Daly had chosen the Christmas play, a prose adaptation of *The Nutcracker*, and was ready to cast it. Naturally I wanted to be Clara; naturally so did Regan.

Mrs. Daly said she was going to run the auditions in a professional way; everyone who wanted to try out for a part had to read cold from the script. No one had seen the script, and Mrs. Daly wouldn't let anyone see it, so no one knew the lines, and she never gave two people the same lines to read, so being last didn't help. Everyone, of course, knew the general idea of the story and could more or less try for some kind of character interpretation, but that didn't keep one from stumbling over the words.

Regan was one of the first to read for Clara and, of course, did beautifully. She didn't stumble once; it was as if she had already memorized the part and rehearsed a month. During her audition, I read the part of the mother. I didn't want to be the mother, but someone had to read the fill-in lines for Regan, and Mrs. Daly gave the job to me. I knew better than to deliberately goof up, I didn't want the teacher—the director in this case—to get the idea I didn't take theater seriously. So I did a good job, too. As good as I could, which from my viewpoint was just as good as Regan, but she had the better lines. This was her audition, after all.

When, late in the class period, it was my turn to try out for Clara, Daniel as the Prince, the Nutcracker, was to read the cue lines for me. I felt lucky. With him on stage with me, I would feel comfortable . . . as soon as we got started . . . because as usual, as we climbed the steps, I had the customary quota of queazies in my stomach.

"You'll do fine," Daniel whispered to me and gave me an encouraging wink.

"You too," I said.

We did okay. Better than adequate. My voice quavered and shook on the first couple of lines, but then it straightened out. When we came off the stage, Mrs. Daly complimented us on a fine job.

Then the tryouts were over, and Mrs. Daly said she would announce the cast the next day.

I was so worried about whether I would get the part that I couldn't work with words with the little kids that afternoon. I let them each pick out an animal to imitate in pantomime, and the rest of us had to guess which animal it was. We had a dozen cats or dogs; a few horses; a tiger and a lion that looked exactly the same to me, but the performing kids were adamant about which role they played; and a snake that was the easiest of all to guess. We had only one snake.

That day I got paid. As usual, I stuck my pay in the bank. I knew I had enough for fare to New York now—unless the price of a ticket had gone up—and that made me excited and happy, but I had to find out what was going to happen about the Christmas play.

I should have known.

Shortly after class began the next day, Mrs. Daly quieted us; we were making anticipatory cast lists to one another.

"I want each of you to know," she said, "that you did well in the auditions and that the players I have chosen were chosen for many reasons, not just excellence in acting. As you know, appearance has a strong influence. So does how one actor will look with another actor on stage. For example we couldn't have a five-foot-six Romeo cast opposite a six-foot-tall Juliet. It wouldn't look right, and the essence of the story would be lost. We would have a comedy instead of a tragedy."

The idea of that made some of the kids laugh.

"Since the Nutcracker is the most important role," Mrs. Daly went on, "first of all I'll announce who will play that role."

A hush fell over the room.

"Daniel Hanbury," she said.

He was sitting next to me, and I heard him take in his breath sharply; he looked at me and smiled kind of tentatively, as though he was a little afraid of the responsibility of being the title character. A few moans came from other students.

"Don't be disappointed," Mrs. Daly said. "Many of you did just as well as Daniel, but as I told you, appearances on stage count, and my Clara is a tall girl, so I had to select a taller Nutcracker."

Dan took my hand. I was one of the tallest girls in class and he probably thought I would get the role.

"Clara will be played by Regan Relaford."

I felt a funny sensation all over my body as if somehow every bit of my strength had leached away and I had the twenty-four-hour virus condensed and encapsulated in a single minute. I don't know when I'd ever felt worse. As soon as that sensation left, I was embarrassed. Privately embarrassed at myself for ever thinking or hoping I would get the part. And then I got mad. My heart seemed to be pounding right in my ears, and for a few moments I couldn't hear anything.

Gradually, I came back to being pretty much myself and could feel Dan squeezing my hand. I glanced at him, and he was looking at me. I lifted my shoulders and turned my eyes away so he couldn't see them. They felt hot, and I was sure they had become horribly bloodshot.

Mrs. Daly was still reading the cast of characters. I was to be the Rat Queen.

The *Rat* Queen!

It was testimonial to my acting ability that I did not let what I was feeling show on my face; if an Oscar had been awarded for that day, I would have won it. I congratulated Regan, and she thanked me graciously, sweetly and modestly. Oh, she was so wonderfully perfect that I could have punched her out! As I was leaving the classroom, Mrs. Daly stopped me.

"It was difficult for me, uh, Tree," she said, "to decide which of you two girls would play Clara. You both were excellent in the tryouts. Don't think my decision was made on ability or training alone. She looks more the part. Her face is rounder, more youthful looking, and you have those marvelous, mature cheekbones."

Thanks, Ma, I thought.

"As you know, I'm assigning understudies for the more important roles, and I would like you to understudy Clara. I'll have an understudy for you, should something happen that might prevent Regan from playing the female lead."

Like a broken leg, I hoped. "All right, Mrs. Daly," I said.

"I know learning two parts will be more work for you, but that won't hurt you—it'll help you."

"Yes, ma'am." She would find out soon enough that I wasn't going to be around to play either the Rat Queen *or* Clara. I had enough money now, and I was going to New York City no matter what anyone said.

"The play we'll be doing in the spring has a lead that might just as well have been written for you, Tree. If you keep working the way you have been, I have no doubt but that you'll be playing the part, so don't worry too much about losing the role of Clara to Regan."

"I won't," I said. I wouldn't be around in the spring, and that was for certain.

"Daniel," she said to Dan who was with me and as far as I could tell knew as little about how I felt or what I was thinking as did the teacher, "I'm asking Roger Stevick to understudy your part." She smiled and started to leave. "I guess I'd better tell him before he gets away."

"How about that?" Dan said to me after she'd left. "Can you believe I have to learn all those lines?"

"You can do it."

"Will you help me? You have to learn Clara's part, too." He put his arm around me and hugged. "I'm glad you're going to understudy Regan. We'll get to be on stage together at least during rehearsal."

"No we won't," I said. "Understudies rehearse with other understudies. I'll be on stage with Roger."

"Are you sure?"

"I'm sure."

He frowned. "That doesn't seem right. What if something did happen to Regan and you ended up being Clara?"

"Nothing will," I said. And I knew nothing would— unless I lured her in front of a car or something. Maybe Jamie would run over her for me.

I knew that wasn't a proper train of thought, but I was so envious that I could have died.

"You don't feel bad that you didn't get the part of Clara, do you?" Dan asked.

"Do I act as though I feel bad?" I asked rhetorically. At least I didn't lie.

He smiled and gave me another one-armed hug. "That's my girl."

The bell rang and we dashed in different directions for our next classes.

That afternoon when Dan drove me to work, I had him stop by the bank and I withdrew my money. While the kids were having a snack of milk and cookies, the first thing they did each day, I approached my boss to verbally tender my resignation.

"Mrs. McQuaide," I said, "I'm going to New York."

"That's nice, dear."

"I mean, I'm moving there."

She looked inquiringly at me.

"I'm going to live with Mom. I'm going to study drama."

"I thought you were doing that here."

"I am, but I think I'll learn more there."

"The schools are that different?"

"Maybe I'll join a group. Take private lessons."

"Won't that cost an awful lot?"

I hadn't thought much about that. Maybe it would. I'd have to ask Dad to help me out. Or Mom. Or both. But then again, maybe I wouldn't have to take lessons, maybe I would land a part in an Off-Broadway production where I could learn on the job. "I thought I ought to let you know I'm leaving."

"When?"

"I thought I'd go after this session. That'll give you time to find someone to replace me."

"You're leaving in the middle of the term? Your parents agreed to that?"

Quickly I looked away from her and at the kids sitting around the tables; for once they were behaving like angels—no one was snitching another's cookie, no one was spilling milk, no one was misbehaving even in the slightest way—so I didn't have any excuse to leave the conversation.

Mrs. McQuaide said, "You haven't discussed this with your parents, have you?"

"No, but that won't make any difference."

"Perhaps not," she said, "but let's discuss this after you've talked with them. Perhaps you'll decide to stay, and if you do, I want you to keep your job. I was thinking that during the next six weeks, you could help the children with crafts. I have many patterns and directions for gifts they could make to give at Christmas. They'd like that."

"Mrs. McQuaide," I said, "I *am* going to leave."

"I know. I remember when I was about your age I was going to move to California and become a flower child. That was all the rage then. I told everyone I was going, and I meant it. But I couldn't do it. Oh, I had the money for the trip, but I wasn't old enough to get a decent full-time job, and the idea of living hand-to-mouth after I got there didn't appeal to me very much. California was the lure, not the other, and I realized if I got my education first, I would be able to support myself. So that's what I did, and I did get to California, though a little later than I'd anticipated." She smiled. "And I'm glad I waited. That's where I met Mr. McQuaide and I might not have done that earlier. He was no flower child." She patted me. "So let's put off talking about you quitting your job until after you have firmer plans. Okay, Tree?"

"My plans are firm," I said.

"I hope you change your mind. I won't start looking for anyone yet."

Well, I'd warned her. What more could I do?

As soon as I got home, I phoned Jamie to see if she would drive me to the airport so I could buy my ticket. I thought again about Mom's car in the garage doing nothing and wished I'd had time to get a license; that way I could have just borrowed the car and driven myself and wouldn't have had to impose on someone else.

I told Dad I was going out with Jamie, but I didn't tell him where I was going. He'd learn soon enough.

"You're crazy," Jamie said to me. "Why are you making me drive you way out to the airport when you don't even know if your folks will let you live in New York? Why didn't you just phone for a reservation?''

"Because if I have a ticket in my hand they won't be able to stop me," I said. "They'll know I mean business."

"They're the ones who'll mean business."

"You don't know, Jamie. You just don't know," I said. And then all the hurts I'd kept so carefully from Daniel came pouring out. I told Jamie everything that had happened in drama class, everything I'd felt, everything Mrs. Daly had said. It took me all the way to the airport to get it out of my system.

"But Mrs. Daly all but promised you the lead in the spring play," Jamie said when I was through.

"That's not the point. The point is if I had studied where Regan has studied, I wouldn't have to wait till spring."

"But you said Mrs. Daly said Regan looked the part more than you did, and that was a deciding factor."

"She just said that to save my feelings."

"Mrs. Daly? Baloney. Who else did she say it to?"

"I didn't listen to her talk to anyone else. For all I know, she said it to everyone." I saw the Delta sign. "Stop here. I won't be but a minute. You can wait out front."

"And have the police get after me?"

"Then make a loop and come back," I said and slammed the door. "I'll wait for you."

There was a line and I had to wait inside, too. But I got my ticket; I would be leaving on Saturday of the next week.

Outside again, I had to wait so long for Jamie that I thought she'd deserted me or had a wreck. But she finally showed up and I waved the ticket at her. "Where've you been?" I asked as I got in.

"Where have *you* been?" she countered. "I had to go around twice."

"There was a long line."

"I wonder if it will be as long when I have to bring you back to get a refund."

"Don't be such a pessimist," I said. "Mom and Dad will let me go."

"The way they did a couple of months ago?"

"This time will be different."

"Can I watch you tell your father?"

I gave her a withering glance. "No. Anyway, I'm going to phone Mother first. She'll understand better than Dad will, and I'll let her tell him."

As soon as I got home, I took the phone into another room and dialed Mom's number and let it ring a dozen or more times, but I didn't get an answer. I tried again in an hour and got the same results. None.

I tried two more times that night and then again in the morning before Dad got up. There still was no response, so I had the operator check to see if Mom's phone was out of order. It wasn't. Where could she be?

Of course Jamie wanted to know what had happened. Of course I told her. And I asked her not to tell anyone I was going to leave. I wanted to do that myself after everything was set up.

Mrs. McQuaide didn't mention my resignation, and neither did I. My ticket was still in my shoulder bag and I could have shown it to her, but I didn't. And the moment I got home, I dialed Mom again. She still didn't answer.

"Dad," I said, traipsing the phone back into the living room, "where's Mom?"

"In Paris," he said.

"Paris!"

"She went to an art exhibit."

"An art exhibit!"

"She had a few of her paintings accepted."

"How long will she be gone?"

"What difference does it make? New York, Paris. She said she would let me know when she got back to the States."

"But how long? Didn't she give you some idea?"

"A month or so."

"A month!"

"What's the matter, Duchess? Did you need her for some special reason?"

"I need her to be in New York so I can move in with her."

"She'll be back in time for your trip at Christmas."

"I'm not talking about Christmas. I'm talking about now."

He narrowed his eyes. "I thought we'd been over this."

I took the phone with me as I left the room. I knew better than to argue my case with as little strength on my side as I had.

Again out of Dad's hearing, I phoned Beaker. If I could get him to let me stay with him, maybe Dad would listen to reason.

Beaker, however, didn't exactly lay out the welcome mat. "I don't have the space," he said. "I finally had to advertise for a roommate so I could make ends meet. If I had known you wanted to rent part of my place, I would have saved the room for you. But I didn't know."

Rent. I couldn't afford to rent. I could barely afford to get up there.

"Why don't you stay with your mother?" he asked.

"She's out of town."

"You could stay in her apartment, couldn't you?"

I hadn't thought of that. "Of course I can," I said. "I think I can. See you later, Beaker. Thank you."

This time before I went into the living room, I got my ticket. "I'm leaving next Saturday," I told Dad and handed it to him.

"'Fraid not," he said.

"I can stay in Mom's apartment. She won't mind."

"Not alone, you can't."

"But, Dad—"

"Teresa, we've been through this before and you know my decision. You also know your mother's decision. You will stay here until you graduate from high school. Then we'll see."

"But I have my ticket," I wailed. "I bought it."

"And I'm proud of you for earning enough money, but you'll have to trade for a fare closer to Christmas." He smiled. "I'm sure that's a one-way ticket."

"It is."

"That can be remedied. I'll add to the price so you can get a round-trip. I'll handle changing it, if you like."

"Go ahead," I said. It wouldn't do him any good to get me a round-trip ticket. The next time I set foot in New York City I wasn't going to set foot out.

# Chapter Six

The hardest thing I had to do was tell Jamie she had been right. Again. The second hardest was to tell Mrs. McQuaide I had changed my mind and wouldn't be leaving after all. Neither of them made me feel any worse than I already felt.

Now all I had to do was get through November and a little more than half of December. And be a rat queen.

It wasn't as easy as I thought it would be.

The six-week session of drama at the day-care center got over and the next week I was to begin teaching simple crafts. Dan picked me up after work.

"I've got some bad news," he told me the moment we were underway and heading down the tree-lined street toward my house.

"I've had a lot of practice handling that sort of stuff," I said. "I'm a pro. So tell me."

"I quit my job."

For a moment I was quiet, waiting for him to explain, but he didn't; he just concentrated on the road. "So?" I prompted.

"So I won't be able to take you to work, or pick you up afterward."

The weather was gradually getting cooler and wetter and if I'd ever needed a ride it would be more welcome now than before. I really should have done something about getting my driver's license. "Why did you quit?"

"Time," he said. "I just don't have time anymore."

"Why not?" I asked before I thought.

"Too much schoolwork." He glanced at me. "If I have to play the Nutcracker, I want to do it well. I don't want to let the class down. Or the school."

Or Regan, I silently added.

"You know I haven't had much experience learning lines," he said. "And with all my other homework, and you know everyone has to help build the sets for the play—well, I have to have the afternoon hours."

"To study," I said.

"I want to get into a decent college, and to do that I have to keep my grade point high."

"I understand," I said, and I did—in one way. I recalled Regan wanting to practice on our one-act during the afternoons; I'd put her off and we'd rehearsed at night. But for this major production, the drama class had to be at the school three nights a week to work on the props and sets and costumes and lighting. If she and Daniel were going to work every day the way she and I had, they would have to do it in the afternoons. In another way I didn't understand. I had to learn two parts, rehearse both of them, do all my other homework and be at the school those three nights just as Daniel did. And I hadn't quit my job.

I looked at him closely and wondered if he were falling for Regan. Everyone else in school had in one way or another, and he might be doing it, too.

He flashed me a quick smile. "I'm glad you understand," he said. "I feel bad about leaving you in the lurch. You'll be able to get to the day-care center all right without my help, won't you?"

"Sure I will. No problem."

"That's good."

"I'll probably get my driver's license."

"That's good," he said again. "You need one."

Maybe for a month and a half I would. After that I wouldn't. "I sure do," I said.

He stopped in front of my house and turned to me. "I'm going to miss seeing you every afternoon, Tree. You aren't angry with me about the change in schedule, are you?"

"Oh, heavens no," I said, and probably would have won an Emmy if one had been offered.

"We'll still see each other in school," he said. "And especially in drama class."

I nodded, but I knew better than that. He would be seeing Regan in drama class a lot more than he would be seeing me. I opened my door and got out. "Thanks for the ride," I said and made myself smile. "Soon as I get my license, I'll give you a ride sometime."

"That's a date," he said.

And that was the only date he asked for. He drove away without another glance in my direction, and for all I knew without another thought, either.

Dad was home, which was good. "Dad, I want to get my unrestricted driver's license," I said first thing.

"I wondered when you were going to get around to that," he said.

"You'll sign the consent?"

"In a second, Duchess. In a second. When do you want to take the test?"

"I'll phone for an appointment and let you know," I said.

"Any time you set it up, I'll take off from work so you can have me along for the trip downtown."

"Thanks, Dad."

I took the first opening they had, which was early in the morning the next Thursday. I got a pass to be late for school that day, and Dad didn't have to get off work; like me, he just had to be late. But he didn't have to get an excuse: he owned his business.

The written test wasn't too hard, and I passed easily. I was a little nervous for the driving test, but I passed that, too. Dad was more pleased than I was. "Now I don't have to worry about driving your mother's car," he said. "It'll get plenty of exercise without me."

I grinned at him. "You bet."

I hadn't told Jamie where I was going that morning, so at noon I suggested that instead of eating in the lunchroom we go to a burger joint. "My treat," I said.

"What's the occasion?"

"You'll see."

She headed for her car, but I steered her to mine. "Oh," she said when she realized what I'd done. "You rat!"

"*Queen* Rat," I said dryly.

"I thought you were going to let me know when you decided to get your license. I was going to go with you."

"It was sort of a quick decision," I told her. "And Dad wanted to take me. Get in. Where do you want to go?"

"To the beach."

"Don't be silly. We have class in forty-five minutes."

"It's only fifteen miles."

"And what would we do when we got there? Turn around and come back?"

"Buy a hamburger and then turn around and come back," she said. "How much gas do you have?"

"Enough."

She glanced around. "Where's Daniel? Isn't he going with us?"

I fired up the engine. "Haven't seen him," I said. And I hadn't seen him alone since the last time he'd driven me home. I'd seen him at lunch and in drama class, but there Mrs. Daly was blocking the play and he was always on stage. Except, of course, when I was. He wasn't in but one scene with the rats, and that was the last one when he fought the king of the rats to protect Candyland for the Sugar Plum Fairy.

"You two haven't had a fight, have you?" Jamie asked.

"No." I let that word rest on its own until we reached Atlantic Boulevard, then I said, "It's just that he's so busy now. And so am I."

"That's one reason I don't like theater," she said. "It takes more time than anything I know."

"But it's worth it."

"If you like it."

I had to let that remark conclude the conversation. I couldn't argue with that.

Jamie and I shouldn't have tried to make it to Jacksonville Beach during the lunch hour; the traffic was fierce and held us up. I let her off at the door so maybe she wasn't tardy, but I was a few minutes late getting to drama class. Rehearsal had already begun. Daniel and Regan were on stage, and they were blocking the final scene.

I sat glumly in the audience with the rest of the rats and the tin soldiers and the other toys. And the longer I sat, the glummer I got. For a first walk-through, I'd never seen such poise and perfection. Neither Daniel nor Regan hesitated in the slightest or showed the tiniest bit of embarrassment at having to embrace. Most high-school kids would have scuffed their toes or giggled or at least blushed, but not those two. They went at it like two Hollywood stars getting a million per film.

As soon as class was over, I beat it out of there. That was the first day I was really glad Dan didn't drive me to work anymore. I did not want to see him. I didn't want to see Regan. To tell the truth, I didn't want to see anyone.

But I couldn't avoid it. That night was the first time we were to work on the technical side of the production, and everyone from class was supposed to report. I thought about playing hooky, but if I did, any edge I had from doing the Halloween play would be wiped out. Possibly that much more would be deducted.

I reported.

Mrs. Daly had a roster posted; it told who was on which crew. I was assigned to set-building. Swell. I'd held a hammer maybe once before in my life. Daniel was to work with props, and Regan was in costuming. At least they wouldn't be together on tech nights.

Fortunately, the head of my crew, who was also the set designer, knew how to hold a hammer. He also knew how to teach the dolts among us how to hold them, too. Before the second week was over, I could hit a nail with the first blow almost every time. By then, of course, most of the nails were driven and it was time to paint the canvas. That was easier for me. A paintbrush doesn't weigh as much as a hammer, and you can sort of sneak up on what you want to paint. If you make a mistake, you can cover it up with the next brush stroke or with a different color, which is totally unlike a hammer—if you don't hit the nail right, it bends, and you have to pull it out and start all over again.

During the time I was learning about set construction I took notes like crazy in drama class, marking exactly where Clara was supposed to move and when, and memorized the lines for that part and for the part of the Rat Queen.

I worked with Daniel one time. On the first Saturday after the cast was announced he wasn't busy, and we cued each other. Then he vanished.

At least as far as I could tell he vanished. He didn't show up in the lunchroom for lunch—he appeared only in drama class. And then we rarely spoke.

I knew where he was most of the time, too. He was with Regan. She had been gung ho to practice our one-act all the time, and I could imagine she was much worse about this major production. The two of them probably got together every afternoon. Every night.

"Jamie," I said one lonely day in mid-November, "do you know where Dan goes for lunch now?"

She looked at me curiously. "Don't you know?"

I hissed air through my teeth. "If I knew, would I ask you?"

"How should I know where he is?"

"I thought somehow, on your way to the lunch-room, since you come from a different direction, you might have seen him."

"But you and Dan are the item around here, not him and me."

"We're not an item."

"Do you want to go look for him?"

"Of course not. I just wondered, that's all."

The next day at lunch, she behaved strangely. She wouldn't look me in the eye and if I mentioned Dan or Regan or drama, she changed the subject to football or homework or the weather; stuff we rarely talked about. She got pretty obvious.

Finally, I caught on. "You found out where Dan goes at noon, didn't you?" I said.

She tried to look innocent and tried again to change the topic of conversation, but I wouldn't let her off the hook.

"Tell me, Jamie."

"I don't think you want to know."

"Tell me."

"You don't get jealous of him?"

"Why should I get jealous?"

"I just wanted to make sure." She lifted her shoulders. "I saw him with Regan."

"So? They were probably rehearsing."

"Yeah. Probably." She began to play with her food instead of bolting it down the way she usually did, and I knew she hadn't told me everything.

"Weren't they?" I asked.

"Probably."

"What were they doing?"

"Rehearsing. I guess."

"Now, Jamie, you're making me angry being so mysterious. Were they rehearsing or were they not? What were they doing? Why don't you just come out with it."

"Well, all right," she said, and her eyes flashed as though maybe she was angrier than I was. "He had his arms around her and they looked really cozy."

A wash of dismay swept over me, but I tried to recoup. "There's a scene in the play near the end where they embrace," I said. "They were most likely working on that."

"He's taking that play seriously, isn't he," she said dryly. "And he's enjoying it an awful lot, as far as I can see."

"He wants to make a good grade."

"Sure he does." Her eyes flashed again. "But it makes me mad. Here I thought he liked you, really liked you, and then I see him snuck off in a dim corner hugging Regan. Makes me lose my faith in human nature."

This was the first I'd heard about a dim corner. Regan and I had never rehearsed in a dim corner.

I told myself it wasn't important. If he wanted to be with Regan, let him; I had only one plan in my life and that was to be an actress. And I didn't have to hang in there but a few more weeks, then I would move north and what Daniel did or didn't do would be way out of my mind.

That's what I tried to think.

But I was jealous.

I didn't let Jamie see.

My acting abilities were getting a better workout off stage than on.

But, finally, I got to be on. The understudies had to go through their paces on stage. Roger was okay. He was nice and good-looking and almost as tall as Daniel, but, let's face it, he wasn't Dan. When we had to rehearse that final scene, I tried to be as cool and casual as Regan and Dan had been, and I think I succeeded, but Roger was the scuffing-his-toes, embarrassed, blushing type. And everyone in class laughed at us. That made *me* embarrassed, and we had to do the scene a dozen times before we got it half as good as the other two had on the first try.

And then later, to top everything off, I had to work with Regan to be sure I had Clara's moves down right. Did I get to work with Daniel who probably knew as much about where to move as Regan did? No. He worked with Roger.

But I was pleasant. Pleasant and cooperative and polite. All I wanted to do was get through the next few weeks with as little difficulty as possible, and while I was at it I figured I might as well learn as much as I could so I'd have a better chance when I got to New York. And everyone, especially Daniel, said Regan knew more about acting than anyone except maybe Mrs. Daly, so this time I deliberately set out to learn as much from her as I could.

Any pointers she had, I absorbed. I worked as hard as I knew how to work. I wiped all extraneous matters from my mind and my life. My homework was done efficiently and competently, and I tended to my job effectively, but the rest of the time—every bit of it—I spent on learning how to act.

It was during this furor of concentration that I realized that though I did indeed have some talent for the craft, I was woefully untrained. That, I knew, could be corrected. And I wanted it corrected within the next few weeks.

You know why.

By the time our production was presented to the public, I knew every move of my part, every move of

Regan's. I knew each nuance of interpretation for both roles. But did Regan get sick or break a leg? No. She was as healthy as could be and I didn't get to be anyone but the Rat Queen.

But I was good. Each night we gave the performance, I got a round of applause as I exited the stage.

Dad thought I was marvelous. Even Regan said I did well. And Daniel flattered me. Sort of. Considering. He said if I kept on working the way I had been, then before too long I would be as good as Regan.

And this time on my report card I got an A. Wouldn't you know that Regan got an A + .

Boy, would I be glad to get to New York!

# Chapter Seven

Y ou aren't serious about staying in New York, are
you?" Jamie asked as she turned onto the approach
road.

She was driving me to the airport terminal once
again, but this time I had my ticket and permission and
I was going to be on the one-thirty plane. Dad would
have brought me, but he had to show a hot client a
house or two, so I'd said goodbye to him this morning.
I hadn't said anything to him about not coming back.
Jamie was the only one who knew that.

"I'm serious," I said.

"You won't like it," she told me. "It's cold up
there."

"It's cold down here."

"Not as."

"Cold is cold."

She was quiet a moment, then she said, "They'll think you talk funny. They'll make fun of your accent."

"I don't have an accent. *They* do. And anyway, I'm working on my diction."

"You'll get mugged," she said, trying a new tack.

I laughed. "Good grief, Jamie, I didn't know you were paranoid. Why would anyone mug me? Do I look rich?"

"It isn't necessary to be rich," she said. "In that city they mug everyone."

"No they don't. That's just bad press. I was there all summer and didn't get mugged."

"Huh. You were lucky."

She recognized the ridiculousness of her statement and this time we laughed together.

"Well, I'm going to miss you," she said.

"Now you're talking about something I can relate to. I'm going to miss you too, Jamie," I told her, and added, "That's about the only reason I can think of that will make staying there less than perfect."

She drove into the short-term parking area and stopped. "What about Daniel?" she asked.

"What about him?"

"Won't you miss him?"

That was a question I didn't particularly want to answer. I got out of the car and reached for my small suitcase that was in the back seat. "Do you want to lock up?"

"I guess I should." She locked the doors, then unlocked the trunk so I could get the rest of my gear. I had a lot of it. I was going to be gone a long time. Like forever.

Both her hands were loaded and so were both of mine as we went into the terminal. "How are you going to handle all this luggage after you land?" she asked. "You'll be alone."

"I'll hire help."

We slipped the bags onto the pass-over and I presented my ticket and was assigned a seat.

"What about Daniel?" she asked again as we went toward the waiting area.

I repeated, "What about him?"

"Well, for one thing, why isn't he here?"

I shrugged. "As far as I know, he doesn't know I'm leaving today."

"He doesn't?" She sounded more surprised than I'd ever heard her sound. "Didn't you tell him?"

"No."

"You haven't? Why not?"

"I haven't seen him lately."

"Why not?"

"That's a question I'm afraid you're going to have to ask him because I don't know." I paused. "For sure."

"But you have your suspicions."

I didn't help her out.

"Regan," she said.

I nodded.

"So they *weren't* rehearsing."

"I don't know if they were or not," I said. "I never asked him and he never volunteered the information."

"But you've *seen* him since then, haven't you?"

"Sure I have."

"And you didn't ask?"

I snorted. "Of course not. Would you have?"

She was quiet a minute, then she said, "I get your point."

"Anyway," I said, "It doesn't matter." I was determined to make myself believe that. I hugged Jamie. "I've got to go. My plane will be boarding in a few minutes. You'll come see me when I get a place of my own, won't you?"

"You know I will."

We both burst into tears and hugged each other again. "I'm going to miss you," I said.

"Me too. You'll write, won't you?"

"You know I will." I broke away from her and all but ran to the concourse that led to my gate. It had been easier to say goodbye to Dad.

I was still sniffing and wiping my eyes when the plane touched down in Atlanta, but I had quit by the time we got to the Newark Airport. I was too excited to be sad.

A redcap helped me move my stuff to the stop where I could catch the bus to the Port Authority in New York City. On the phone I'd told Mom I would make my own way to her place; neither she nor I saw any sense in her coming all the way to New Jersey. I wasn't a child, after all.

After the bus arrived, I stowed my stuff in the luggage carrier and got on and shortly we were under way. It was dusk, almost dark, but I could see the lights of the city get closer and closer, and I watched them as if I were mesmerized. My heartbeat increased to maybe twice its normal rate. I loved this place. Even the stink of the tunnel was like rare perfume; it spoke of busyness, traffic, haste, congestion.

And then I was in Manhattan.

Nobody on the bus was as thrilled as I was. No one could have been.

I looked around for someone I could tell; I was bursting and had to let out some of my feelings or explode. The woman across the aisle didn't look away when I caught her eye, and I smiled at her.

"I'm moving up here," I said.

"You like New York?"

I smiled wider. "More than anything."

"I like it, too," she said. "I'm always glad to get home from a trip."

"I've come to visit my Mom, but I'm going to stay," I said. My entire life story tumbled out of my mouth between then and when the bus bounced and jostled around the bends into the terminal and stopped. Whoever said New Yorkers weren't friendly didn't know what they were talking about; I hadn't met any more than the average percentage of rushed or rude people there than I had anywhere.

"Is your mother meeting you?" the woman asked as we got off the bus.

"No. I'm going to catch a taxi."

"Which way are you headed? Maybe we could share."

"Downtown. To the Village."

"Too bad," she said. "That's opposite from me."

She had only one suitcase, and she helped me get my gear to the sidewalk, so I let her have the first available cab. And then I had to wait. This was the rush hour and every cab I saw already had a passenger. I would have taken the subway, but I had too much stuff.

Finally I got a ride. The driver helped me load my bags, and because of the traffic I had a chance to look at the little stores we passed. There were hundreds, and most of them had some kind of Christmas decoration. I decided I would walk all the way up Fifth Avenue the next day and look at everything.

Then the taxi stopped in front of a gloomy, not too tall building; not very many buildings in the Village were tall. The place looked familiar to me. It looked like home.

I tipped the taxi driver royally for helping me get my things to the entry; I felt rich. I hadn't spent a cent out of my last paycheck from Mrs. McQuaide, and I had some left over from the first two because all I'd spent out of those was enough for half a ticket. Of course I hadn't bought anyone a Christmas present yet. But I had plenty.

Not two minutes after I buzzed Mom's apartment, she flew down the steps and opened the door and grabbed me. "Teresa!" She hugged me so tight that I couldn't breathe, but I was hugging her back just as hard and she probably couldn't, either.

We didn't break each other's ribs, though. We stopped short of that and stood back and looked at each other. I swear my mother doesn't look like a mother— maybe an older sister, but not much older. She had on jeans and a patterned sweatshirt, and her hair, blond like mine, was caught behind her ears in a huge barrette that reached from one side of her neck to another.

"I've missed you so much," she said and squeezed me again. "How is your father?"

"He's fine. Have you missed him, too?"

"More than you can imagine. Oh, gosh, I'm glad you're here."

I wanted to tell her I was here to stay, that she wouldn't have to miss me ever again because I wouldn't be gone for her *to* miss, but she was reaching for a couple of my bags. "Goodness," she said with a laugh, "what did you do? Bring your entire wardrobe?"

"Just about." I got the other two suitcases and followed her up the stairs.

"I don't know where we're going to put all your things," she said as she opened the door to the apartment.

I said, "Where we did last time."

Again she laughed. "Yeah. Crammed into the corner."

The place was just as crowded as I remembered, but Mom had added new paintings to the walls and changed others; there was not an empty square foot of wall to be seen. And her work had gotten better.

I dropped my bags and slipped my shoulder-bag strap off and threw the purse on the sofa. "Mom, these are great," I said, going to the nearest paintings. "You really are a terrific artist."

"Flattery accepted."

"That wasn't flattery. It was the truth."

"Well, thank you, Teresa. I guess my work and dedication are paying off."

"Hey, Mom," I said, turning to her, "I wish you'd call me Tree."

"Tree?"

"Yes." I grinned. I hadn't asked Dad to call me that, and it was nearly the first thing out of my mouth to my mom. "I'm changing the spelling of my name to Treesa so it'll be memorable on a marquee."

"It will be. But you know, don't you, honey, that what is behind the name is the thing that matters. If you're good enough, people will remember your name."

"I know. But still . . ."

"Still, every edge helps. Okay, Tree. Did you eat on the plane?"

"No."

"Why don't you unpack while I run down to the corner and get us some Chinese. Would you like that?"

"I'd love it."

She hugged and kissed me again, then put on a parka. She looked even younger than before. "I'll be back in just a few minutes," she said.

I had forgotten how tiny my allotted space was. Not even half my clothes would fit in the section of the coat closet set aside for me. Summer clothes didn't take up nearly as much space as winter ones. I had to shove two of the bags still loaded under my bed.

Mom came back with cartons just as I was finishing, and as we ate I filled her in on news from home. Especially about my traumas in drama class and Regan. "And that was because she got to study here," I said, planning to break the news that Mom had a daughter-guest permanently.

"I don't think at her age the place where she studied was as important as the fact that she did study. And you said she was still at it, pushing, working hard. That's what makes the difference."

"But, Mom," I said, feeling my hopes that she would support my decision going down the tubes.

"You could learn from Regan," she said. "And I don't mean just pointers in acting—you could learn how dedication pays off. It obviously has for her, and it can for you."

"But, Mom—"

"Honey," she said and put her hand over mine. "Let's don't ruin your first evening here. Okay?"

I was beginning to think no one would ever understand. But I backed off. After all, I had two weeks in which to change her mind. "Okay," I agreed.

After we were through with dinner and cleaning up the few dishes we'd dirtied, I asked, "Does Beaker still live here?"

"As far as I know," Mom said.

He lived one floor above Mom, so I ran up and knocked on his door, but he didn't answer.

When I woke up in the morning, I banged my elbow on the bookcase and that made me smile. This time I knew exactly where I was. I was where I ought to be. From where I lay, I once more admired the artwork on the walls. It was a wonder to me that Mom didn't already have things hanging in the Guggenheim. Or the Louvre.

She was already up and at work in her studio. "I'm sorry I have to work, Tree," she said, "but you know me. I've got to keep at this until I get it right."

"It looks to me as if you already have."

"I'm close," she said. "But close only counts when one is playing horseshoes. Can you get along without me?"

"Sure. I haven't done any shopping, and I've got to buy presents for everyone. And I want to look in the windows on Fifth Avenue."

"Maybe this evening we can take in a show. On Broadway. Would you like that?"

"You need to ask?"

"No. That's why I already got tickets."

That earned her another hug from me, then I left her to her work.

It was too early to see if Beaker was home; if he were, he would be asleep and he might kill me for waking him. He almost always slept until noon. Also it was too early for most of the stores to be open, but I mainly wanted to look at windows, anyway.

I bundled up. Jamie was right; it was colder here. But I'd brought every winter outfit I owned, so I was warm enough as I walked past the nearby stores. Everything was Christmassy. Even some of the people. A number of the young people had their hair cropped on one side and spiked on the other, and many of them had colored one half green and the other half red. Their outfits were wild, too. They were as much fun to look at as the windows were. I wondered how they could get the courage to do their hair that way; I didn't think I would ever be that brave.

The farther I walked, the more conservative the clothes got. And I got nearer to the big stores. I decided to hike on up to Macy's, and then I'd cut over to Fifth. If I got tired, I could take a bus or the subway back.

Herald Center was opening its doors when I got there, so I went in and rode the escalators from floor to floor, looking in all the windows of the shops I passed. Then I took the elevator down and went on to Macy's. The window displays were worth the walk. They would have been worth twice the distance. Three times. I must have spent an hour watching the animations; then I spent an equal amount of time inside the store where I found a fabulous scarf I knew Jamie would adore.

I paid to have it wrapped and shipped from there. Even so, she might not get it in time for the big day.

By then, it was past lunchtime and the crowds had grown to mammoth proportions and I was getting tired. If I didn't want to wear myself out on the first day, I would have to save Fifth Avenue until later. Besides, Beaker would be awake and he was my pipeline into the theater. I wanted to see what he was up to and what was going on. Maybe he could help me find a job. Maybe he could think of some good arguments to help sway Mom into letting me stay.

I couldn't believe I'd been gone from home for so long and hadn't bought anything for anyone but Jamie.

It was a toss-up whether I would take the subway or the bus back, and the subway won. The crowds were fierce underground, too. I hadn't seen so many people waiting for trains except the one time last summer when I went for a ride at rush hour just to see how it felt. But it was cold this time and everyone had on bulkier clothes—and they needed them. When the trains came through the tunnels and whooshed that wind around, it was as cold or colder than it was above.

At least that's what I thought until I came out at the other end. It was snowing. Not hard, but any snow was more than we usually got in Jacksonville, which was maybe an eighth of an inch every three years or so.

I wanted to buy skis and go skiing. I wanted to go ice skating. Maybe Mom would go with me to Rockefeller Center.

I ran up the steps. But she was gone. She'd left a note saying she would be back in time for us to have dinner somewhere elegant and then go to the theater. She had been gone a lot while I was visiting her last summer, too, so I was used to it. I could ask her later.

I made myself a sandwich and ate it on the way to Beaker's apartment. He was in, and seemed delighted to see me.

"Come on in. Come on in," he said. "I expected you weeks ago. Why didn't you move into your mom's apartment?"

"Don't ask."

He grinned. "Your folks said you were too young."

I nodded.

"You'll get older. No stopping that. I had to wait till I was eighteen to get to move here and live alone. Parents know what they're talking about."

"Not you too!" I said, feeling betrayed.

"Me too. Sit down. You probably should be sitting down when you hear my news."

"News?"

"Sit."

I did, on the edge of the chair. Just by looking at him, I could tell his news would be about the theater; he was so excited that his eyes sparkled and his face was flushed.

"I'm sitting," I said. "So tell me."

"I got a job."

"Acting!" I shouted without giving him a chance to elaborate. "You're in a play!"

He struck a pose. "Yes, madame. I'm in a play."

"You're working! And you haven't been here but a year and a half. I think that's wonderful. I could die with envy. How did you get the job?"

He collapsed into the chair opposite me. "You wouldn't believe the machinations."

"Where is the play?"

"Off-Broadway."

"Tell me about your part. Do you have any lines? What do you do?"

"I have a few lines. Two or three. That's not many, but it's better than none. I play a waiter."

"Oh, I wish I could get a part," I said, sagging back in my seat. "Even as a walk-on. If I had a job Mom couldn't make me go back and live with Dad."

"She'll make you leave?" He sounded as incensed as I was. "But why? She's back. She's living here. You'd be with her—you wouldn't be alone."

"Try to explain that to them. *I* can't."

"What reasons do they give?"

"Mom is working at being an artist, and Dad wants her to be able to devote all her time to that. If I was around, apparently I'd distract her or keep her from doing her best because she'd worry about me." I sighed. "And that would keep her away from home longer."

"You think if you had a job they'd let you stay?"

"They couldn't keep me from it."

"Well, let's look in *Variety* for a cattle call, then. I don't think anyone is casting plays now, but you never know about movies. Maybe someone needs a special type. One you'd fit." He jumped up and got his copy and spread it on the floor.

I got down beside him and he studied one half of the paper as I studied the other half. Within five minutes, he said, "Here's one."

"Where?"

He pointed at an insert. "We lucked in. The auditions are for tomorrow afternoon, and they'll be cold from the script. And it's for someone about your age." Then he leaned his nose closer to the page and looked dejected. "But it's for a major role, not a bit part."

"I don't care. I'd just as soon have a major role."

He smiled. "Wouldn't we all. But everyone will turn out for the auditions. You'll have hundreds of kids for competition. They'll come from miles away."

I grinned. "I came from miles away."

"You probably won't get the part."

"If I don't try, I certainly won't," I said.

# Chapter Eight

I didn't tell Mother. Oh, I thought about it, and I wanted to, and I almost did a couple of times, but I didn't do it. She might have tried to persuade me not to go because she would think if I didn't get the part I would be terribly unhappy, maybe even crushed. Or she might have stopped me because she would know what I was up to.

So, as excited and nervous and anticipatory as I was, I managed to keep my mouth shut during dinner and the play. And it was a good one. We had seats on the front row of the balcony where I had a clear view of all the action and could hear every word. Afterward, Mom told me she thought a few times that I might fall over the railing because I leaned so far over trying to get closer to the action.

In the morning, she was again in her studio when I awoke. I knew better than to disturb her while she was working, so there was no chance that I would spill the beans then.

I spent the morning getting ready, both psychologically and physically. Never had I spent so much time on makeup, not even when I played the Rat Queen and had to cover my entire face with gray and put on ears and whiskers. And I must have tried on half a dozen outfits before I was satisfied with how I looked.

The snow of the day before had vanished by the time I went out. The tiny bit that had stuck in corners was melted by the warmer air, and the weather was almost balmy. It was easy to get a taxi.

I figured the little bit of extra expense for a cab was worth it; I didn't want to get crushed on a subway or a bus, and I didn't want to walk and look windblown and tired when I tried out. I could walk home. Or float, if I was lucky.

Beaker and I had talked about whether I should go early so I would be one of the first to audition, or whether I should go late and be one of the last. We had decided on early because if as many aspiring actresses showed up as we thought would, by the time the final ones read, the casting director would be worn out with listening and might not hear me even if I was the best all day.

We miscalculated what early meant, or everyone else had the same idea we did. By the time I got there, the anteroom was packed. I'd never seen so many varieties of teenage girls in one place at one time. There were short ones and tall ones, brunettes and blondes, chubby, childlike girls and tall, emaciated types and everything in between. Some were obviously too old and tried to look younger, and some were obviously too young and tried to look older. A few were dressed and made up to look as innocent as Little Bo Peep, and others were so chic and sophisticated that they looked bored by life. Most of them, though, were dressed much the way I was—neat but smart.

When you went in, which was more like forcing and shoving your way in, you were given a form to fill out. Name, address, height, age—stuff like that. There was a section where you were to write what experience you'd had—your credits. I felt kind of funny putting down Rat Queen and the little play I'd written and directed, but I had to put something, meager as it was. I could see on others' pages lists of performances that had to have taken years to amass.

And then we waited.

The forms had been numbered in order of arrival; girls were called one by one into an adjoining room. No one in the waiting room could hear what was going on in there. Some of the contestants were in and out in a minute or two, but others stayed longer. And every one of them when they came out got their stuff if they'd left any and went out without saying a word.

No one who was waiting said much, either. Everyone was at least a little scared. Me included. If I'd thought trying out for Mrs. Daly was nerve-racking, that was nothing compared to this. I began to wish I'd come at dawn so I could have been one of the first to read and have it over with. And it didn't help to hear the numbers called get closer and closer to mine.

Then one girl came out and didn't leave; her expression wasn't as woebegone as those before her, either. She resumed her seat—by now with the thinning of the crowd everyone had one, but she didn't say anything. Everyone looked at her, and I had to admire the way she studiously kept information from showing. We all knew what had happened, though. She'd been asked to stay. She was a finalist.

There were only three ahead of me when my stomach began to growl. I'd been too excited to think about eating breakfast, and it was past lunchtime. I hoped no one except me could hear it, but the girl next to me glanced at me and smiled. "Me too," she said.

Two to go. My stomach got so full of butterflies that it gave up asking for food.

One.

My hands got cold and sweaty.

Then my number was called.

"Break a leg," the girl next to me whispered.

I murmured, "Thanks," and got up. I tried not to wobble as I crossed the room, and as far as I could tell, I appeared calm and confident.

But inside the room, a woman stood up to shake hands with me and it's a wonder my grip didn't give her frostbite.

"Don't be nervous," she said.

My throat had quit working, so I couldn't speak up and lie by telling her I wasn't.

"Sit over there and read this," she said, and handed me a couple of worn pages.

As I moved to the chair she had indicated, I glanced over the lines and swallowed a few times to remind my throat it had to help me. What I read didn't tell me much about the character.

"Conversational," the woman said. "The character is trying to convince her parents she is old enough to leave home."

I grinned. "That should be easy," I said and was relieved to find my vocal apparatus hadn't quit on me.

"I hope so." She gestured for me to begin.

For the first sentence, my voice did its insecure trick of quavering and I thought if I were truly professional I wouldn't quaver. Regan wouldn't quaver. If I were talking to my own mother and father I wouldn't quaver. And it straightened out.

By the time I got to the final lines, I was into the part and was doing a pretty good job. I could tell this character wasn't having much more luck than I had, so I ended with a sort of whine.

"Thank you," the woman said, and I looked at her; she was fingering the form I'd filled out. "You haven't had much experience, have you?"

"No," I admitted.

"You need to get more."

I wondered how I was going to do that if people didn't give me the opportunity.

"I hesitate to ask you to stay and read with the finalists because I don't think you're going to be exactly right for this part," she said. "But then again—"

"I'll stay," I all but shouted.

"You'll probably be wasting your time."

"I don't care. I don't have anything else to do." My heart was going like a trip-hammer. "Not one thing." I wondered if my note to Mother would cover being gone another couple of hours, and decided it would have to.

"All right," the woman said, "if you'll take a seat in the waiting room again, we shouldn't be too much longer."

Though I tried, I know as I went back into the other room I wasn't as successful at making my face a blank as the other girl had been; I could feel my eyes dance.

She looked at me as I sat down, and her eyebrow went up a trifle and the edge of her lips twitched.

Only twenty or so girls remained and of those one more was asked to remain. Waiting this time was more difficult than it had been before; I was itching to tell anyone and everyone I had made the finals.

And then the room was empty except for the three who had been asked to wait. All three of us were tall, slim and blond, and I recalled that the brunettes had come out of the smaller room much more quickly than had the blondes. The chubby ones more quickly than that. As Mrs. Daly had said, appearance counted sometimes more than talent.

But I knew that now only talent mattered.

The woman came out of the smaller room and joined us. "I want to see some movement," she said, and put us through our paces. I was glad I'd had the little bit of training I'd had. It came in handy.

We each were asked to read again, a different selection this time, and the woman looked at me. "Treesa," she said, "I was afraid of this."

My heart fell. I knew what she was going to say.

"You have talent, Treesa. There is no doubt in my mind about that, but you haven't had much experience or training."

I nodded. She was right.

"I'm sorry. We won't be able to use you. You need to study. Land some roles. Work. If you do, you'll make it someday."

The other two girls looked at me and I could see sympathy in their eyes, but there was delight, too. One of them would get the part and they knew it.

"Don't feel bad," the woman said to me and patted me on the arm. "You did very well."

I nodded, murmured, "Thank you," grabbed my shoulder bag and stumbled out of there.

I felt such conflicting emotions that I couldn't sort the strongest one out; I was hurt and bleeding, I was proud, I was embarrassed, I was determined, I was destroyed, I was strengthened, I was on the lowest ebb of despair and I was at the height of exhilaration. I was so confused about what I did feel that I stayed stunned in the corridor outside that room for what seemed like a long time, but in my state could have been as short a time as a minute.

What was I going to say to Beaker?

Would I tell my mother what I'd done?

How would Regan have fared if she had auditioned?

What would Daniel think about it?

Wouldn't Jamie think I had a lot of brass to do what I had done?

That thought made me smile, and I was able to move again.

Of course I would tell Mom about my experience, and Beaker would be proud of me for getting as far as I'd gotten, and Regan would have been turned away right away because she has dark hair, and Daniel... I'd lost touch with Daniel. I should write him or send him a Christmas present. We'd been friends too long to drop it without at least saying why.

By the time I got to the street, my feelings had sorted themselves out and the important things had come to the top. I had done my best and I had done well and I should be pleased with myself. And I was.

I was more determined than ever to stay in New York, where I could study.

It was only three long blocks across town, two short blocks down to get to Macy's, and I went and bought a pair of gloves I knew Dan would like. I didn't have to look—I knew right where they were, and I realized that

all the time I'd been shopping for Jamie I'd had him in
the back of my mind. Again I paid to have the package
wrapped and shipped.

I mailed Christmas cards to Mrs. McQuaide and Mrs.
Daly, and in an afterthought, I sent one to Regan, too.
And on the bottom I told her about the auditions and
how far I'd gotten.

It was nearly dark by the time I got home, and Mom
was cooking dinner. The smells made my stomach start
to rumble again, and I remembered I hadn't eaten a
thing.

"Every day I expect to see piles of packages, but you
come home empty-handed," Mom said. "I thought
you'd been Christmas shopping."

"I have. Sort of," I told her. "I sent gifts to Jamie
and Daniel."

"That's nice."

"But I haven't gotten anything for Dad yet," I said.
"Or for you."

"That's not so nice." She grinned at me. "I haven't
done any shopping, either. We're going to have to take
care of that one of these days."

"I haven't done much shopping because I've been
busy doing other things," I said. I was trying to pique
her curiosity, but she'd gone back to stirring what
looked like chili or spaghetti sauce. "Really exciting
things," I added, and still she didn't respond. I put my
hands on my hips and said, "Highly important earthshaking things."

She looked at me again, but she didn't stop stirring.
"Earthshaking? Like what?"

I shrugged, blasé. "Oh, trying out for the lead in a
movie."

She stopped stirring. "Doing *what*?" she asked.

"Well, maybe it wasn't exactly the lead, but it was one of the most important parts."

"And you—" She turned the fire down. "This'll be okay. You come in here and tell me what you're talking about." She took my arm and marched me into the living room and sat me down. "You tried out for a part in a film?"

I nodded.

"Did you get it?"

"Nope," I said, "but I came close."

The story of my day spilled out, and I recounted the events with dramatic intensity. Mom worried when I had worried, feared what I had feared and suffered what I had suffered. When I was through, she said, "Good grief."

"But she said I had promise."

"I know you do."

"She said I had talent."

"You do."

"And she said I should study."

"So you should."

"That's why I want to stay with you, Mom," I blurted. "I want to study here."

"You need to eat," she said and got up and went back into the kitchen. "You haven't eaten all day."

I tagged along behind. "Will you and Dad talk it over again? I can learn so much here."

"Yes you can," she said, stirring again. "And I certainly hope your enthusiasm continues until you're old enough to do just that. If it does, we'll know you're serious."

"I *am* serious."

"Then you'll study where you can."

"Oh! You just don't understand!"

"I don't?" she said. "*I* don't?" She gestured toward her studio. "If anyone in this world can understand, it's me. So don't tell me I don't understand."

"But I want to—"

"And when the time comes, you can. That's a promise. And it is just as binding as the one I made to myself." She started to ladle from the pot to bowls. "Get some spoons."

Dinner wasn't spaghetti sauce or chili as I had thought; it was some weird kind of homemade soup. Mom never was the greatest cook in the world.

After the dishes were done, I went upstairs to tell Beaker what had happened, but he was already gone. To work in his play, I supposed.

I couldn't tell him until the next day, and he was impressed. "I knew you had talent," he said.

Sure. Everyone knew I had talent, but no one would let me do anything with it.

The day before Christmas Eve, Mother and I finally got around to going shopping. This time both of us were heaped with packages as we came home, and we couldn't open the door. We'd gotten in downstairs because someone was going out as we were coming in, but we couldn't expect that at the apartment door.

She looked at me and I looked at her and we giggled. "Who's going to put everything down?" she asked.

"Who has the most?"

"I do."

"I don't think so. I think I do."

"One, two—" She started counting and we giggled like kids again.

And suddenly, the door opened. It was Dad.

"Lamar," Mom said.

"Anita."

They looked at each other a moment, then he took the things out of her arms. "Let me help you."

He was so taken with seeing her and she was so stunned by seeing him that they both forgot me loaded like an early Santa Claus. I staggered inside behind them.

"What are you doing here?" Mom asked.

"I missed you," he said, putting down the packages. "There isn't much business around Christmas, so I closed the office until the New Year and came on up." He looked at her. "I hope you don't mind."

"Mind?" She sounded a lot the way I do on the first few lines of an audition. "Of course I don't mind."

"I won't interrupt your work?"

She waved a hand in dismissal, as if her painting meant little or nothing to her.

Then all of a sudden they were in each other's arms. That made me feel good. I hadn't seen them together for over a year.

I tiptoed to the couch to put down my packages and then made myself scarce.

I knew when I wasn't needed.

Because Dad hadn't bought any presents for anyone we had to go shopping the next day, and let me tell you there wasn't much left to buy, but we bought what there was. All three of us were loaded down when we got home.

We hadn't had such a big Christmas since I was old enough to remember.

The next week we went to all the touristy things in New York City there were to go to. Dad had never been to the city before. We went to the top of the Empire

State Building, we visited the Statue of Liberty, we saw the UN, we went to the planetarium and wandered through the Museum of Natural History and the Museum of Modern Art and the Guggenheim. We rode the Staten Island Ferry and nearly froze to death, and we went to a concert in Central Park and saw a musical.

Dad loved the city as much as Mom and I did.

I was glad. Now that he knew what was here, he would surely change his mind and that would help Mom change hers. I just knew that was what would happen.

We were members of the crowd at Times Square for the New Year's Eve celebration, and while the ball descended I made a resolution to study as hard as I could and learn as much as I could—and do it in this place.

But that was not what Mom and Dad had resolved. Obviously.

The next day, Dad started packing his things and asked me why I wasn't doing the same. "I got a ticket on the same return flight as you," he said. "You'd better get started or we'll be late."

"Dad," I said. "Mom."

They knew me too well. In unison, they said, "Don't start."

"But, listen—"

"If you're getting ready to talk about staying in New York, you can forget it," Dad said.

Mom said, "Tree, we went through this just the other day."

"Tree?" Dad said.

"I don't know what difference a year and a half makes. You both have said I could come here when I'm eighteen. What's magic about eighteen?"

"For one thing, you will have graduated from high school," Dad said.

"But Mom's living here now. She might not be living here by the time I turn eighteen. For all I know she could be living in Paris and I'd have to pay for my own place."

"You can get a job when you're eighteen," Mom put in. "You can't stay now."

"Pack your things, Duchess," Dad ordered.

# Chapter Nine

Everything I owned got packed; Mom helped, Dad helped, even I helped, though I didn't want to.

I thought about running away and wondered what would I do if I did, and then I thought running away wouldn't make me older and I was still too young to get a good job, plus I didn't have my education. Mom and Dad were right about people needing one of those. And I had heard too many sad stories about girls who ran away.

Anyway, what I wanted to do was study acting, and how could I afford to do that or even have time to do it if I had to work all the time? The answer to that was simple: I couldn't. The only way I could have what I wanted was to convince my folks to agree; I had to have their support.

Going back to Florida was much against my will, and my mind was so busy trying to figure out a way to force my parents to let me stay that I didn't remember to tell Beaker I was leaving. I guessed he'd figure it out. At the airport, I did tell my mother goodbye; I was civil enough to do that, but I wasn't civil enough to talk to Dad on the trip home and I know I made the flight unpleasant for him. I know because he told me after we landed in Jacksonville.

We got out of the terminal and headed for the car, and I nearly sweltered in the heavy clothes I'd put on in the morning. It was warm, balmy, like a spring day and not like winter at all. But I didn't want to be in sunny Florida, I wanted to be in New York.

"Do you know how you've been behaving?" Dad said.

I glanced at him.

"Like a spoiled child."

I wanted to defend myself and say I'd been behaving like a mistreated adult, but he didn't pause long enough for me to say anything.

"I've never seen you this way," he went on. "You made your mother very unhappy before we left, and you've made this trip as uncomfortable as possible for me. I never would have thought a daughter of mine would be so stubborn."

"But you didn't—" I started.

"You know your mother and I have your best interests at heart. We know how much you want to be an actress and we want you to be one if that's your desire."

"Then—"

"But you have to take things a step at a time. You can't automatically be the greatest thing the Broadway stage has ever known. You have to earn that."

"That wasn't why I wanted to stay. I wanted to study."

"You know perfectly well that you can do that here." We had reached the car and he unlocked the trunk, flung it open and began to stuff the suitcases in as though each of them were an enemy. "I thought you were more intelligent. I thought you had more sense. Both your mother and I have told you more times than we can count that after you graduate, when you're old enough, you will be allowed to go where you want."

"But Mother's there now. She got to go."

"I know she's there. She earned the right to go." He took off his jacket and threw it in on top of the bags. "She worked for the opportunity." He unlocked the doors to the car. "Get in."

I did. He got behind the wheel and slammed the door. I'd never seen him so angry.

"Now I want you to straighten up and behave like the decent human being I know you are. And I do not, *do not*, want to talk about this anymore. Do you understand?"

"Yes."

"All right," he said more quietly. "All right." He didn't say another word all the way home.

We unloaded the car and I was carefully polite. I hung around the house until the tension between Dad and me had eased a bit, then I asked him if I could drive over and visit Jamie. I didn't want to phone her for two reasons: I didn't want Dad to hear what I had to say and I didn't want to have to admit I had failed in my mission without being close enough to Jamie to hit her if she made fun of me.

"Sure you can go, Duchess," he said, "but don't be gone long. School tomorrow."

"I won't."

I didn't know if Jamie would be home; it was evening and the end of a holiday and she didn't know I was back in town. But I saw both the cars when I drove into the driveway of her house, which was as familiar to me as my own, and maybe more so because she hadn't moved once since I'd met her and we had moved at least six times. Dad was always fixing up our house and selling it. The one we were in then could have been on the market, for all I knew.

Of course someone could have come by and picked Jamie up; she could be off on a date. Maybe she didn't have a steady boyfriend, but she was no wallflower, by anyone's standards.

I knocked on the door and waited, and after I knocked again, nine-year-old Chucky, dressed in jeans and a T-shirt extolling the virtues of his favorite cartoon character, answered and looked at me as if he'd seen a ghost. "I thought you'd moved away," he said, sounding surprised and a little angry. "Jamie said you'd be gone forever. She cried and cried for hours and hours until I nearly barfed."

"I'm sorry about that, Chucky. Is she home?"

"Yeah, she's home," he said, not moving away from where he hung between the door and the facing.

"May I come in?" I asked.

"I don't know," he said. "Are you going to make her cry again?"

"I hope not."

"Well." He drew the word out and didn't move.

"Chucky," I said, "if you don't get out of my way I'm going to pick you up and move you."

He stuck out his chest. "Try it."

"I'm serious. I will."

"I dare you." He had a sparkle in his eyes. "I double-dog dare you."

"Okay."

He had gotten bigger since the last time I'd picked him up, like maybe seven years bigger, but I could still lift him if I used enough effort. And I did and set him aside, but my fingers evidently gouged a rib because he giggled. "I didn't think you could do it," he said.

"I can do anything I set my mind to," I told him. "Where's Jamie?"

"In her room. Should I announce you?"

I looked at him. "What television shows have *you* been watching?"

He giggled again and I left him behind.

I didn't want to scare Jamie into looking at me as though she'd seen a ghost, too, so before I went in I tapped on her door and said, "It's me."

"Who's me?"

She was sprawled on her bed, surrounded by magazines, and was wearing slacks and what was, I swear, the identical T-shirt Chucky had on, but in a larger size. She never did particularly care what she wore. She smiled when she saw me. "Well, well. Look who's here."

"Don't start in," I warned her.

My tone if not my words wiped the smile from her face and she sat up. "What's wrong, Tree?"

"I can't— They don't—" The strain of having to be nice to Dad and the disappointment of having to leave New York and the frustrations at being unable to do anything about that came to an exploding point and I started to cry.

"Teresa," Jamie said, sounding truly concerned. "What happened? What's wrong?"

I shook my head. I was crying so hard that I couldn't talk. I sat down on the bed beside her.

"Is everyone all right?" she asked.

I nodded.

"Your mom? Your dad?"

I nodded again and sobbed out, *"Parents!"* and threw myself across her bed and really let go. I hoped Chucky wouldn't hear me and barf.

Jamie sat beside me and occasionally patted me consolingly and waited for me to get myself under control, which I finally did with much hiccupping and half a box of her Kleenex. "I don't know what I'm going to do," I told her when I could manage my voice enough to speak. "I simply don't know what I'm going to do."

"About what?"

"About *what*?" I shot back at her. "Look at me."

She did. "I'm looking. So?"

"I'm *here*," I wailed.

"You've been here before. What's wrong with being here?"

"I was supposed to be in New York. I want to be in New York. I told you I was going to stay in New York."

"And that's what you've been crying about?"

"What else?"

"Well, I never expected you would stay up there. I expected you'd be back. You told me what your parents said to you, what they'd decided." She grinned and tried to cheer me up. "Don't forget, I have parents, too. I know how they work. Or don't work, as the case may be."

I gave a last hiccup of self-pity and blew my nose. "I am not going to give up," I said. "They just don't understand how important this is to me."

"Are you sure?"

"Am I sure!"

"I mean, maybe they do understand. Maybe they understand more than you think."

"They're ruining my life."

"Are they?"

"What are you?" I asked, getting angry. "A turn-coat? A traitor? An Arnold Benson?"

"A Benedict Arnold."

"Whatever. Are you?"

"No, I'm not a Benedict Arnold, but I think you're pushing a little too hard. I think maybe they might be right. Maybe you ought to continue studying here and learn all you can and then when you're old enough—"

"Bite your tongue." I stood up. "I have not yet begun to fight."

"John Paul Jones," she said.

"Don't rub it in that you're better at history than I am. I'm better at math."

"Maybe a fraction," she said.

Who could stay mad at Jamie?

"Listen," I said, "has anything happened at school? I don't mean at school, but to anyone we know *from* school?"

"Like Daniel?" she asked, looking innocent.

"Well, yeah, like him."

"I haven't seen him."

"At all?"

"Not once."

"And Regan?"

"I haven't seen her, either."

Well, I would see both of them tomorrow. Would they be together?

\* \* \*

Just before lunchtime I spotted Regan in the locker corridor.

"Tree," she said, advancing on me and giving me her dazzling smile. "I got your card. Thank you."

I turned my hand over, indicating that the sending of it had been nothing.

"You actually got to the final reading in the audition," she said, not asking but sounding impressed. "I think that's wonderful. I went to a few tryouts when I lived in New York but I never made it to the finals."

"I was the right type," I admitted.

"Still," she said, "there were probably dozens who were the right type."

"There were."

"Tell me about it."

I did. With as much detail as I could manage while we walked to the lunchroom. Halfway there, Jamie joined us and we went through the line together, and all three of us sat at the corner table. Regan had never sat with Jamie and me before, possibly because I had never asked her. And I kept talking. Jamie listened even though I'd given her an abbreviated version before I left her house the night before. She really didn't have an alternative. But there was no abbreviating for Regan; she threw in questions any time I paused for breath.

Then Daniel showed up and I cut off like a record when the needle lifts.

"Hi," he said warmly, but I didn't know if the warmth was for Regan or for me. He took the vacant chair between us. "Thank you for the gloves, Tree," he said. "That was a nice thought. They fit perfectly."

Again my hand flipped over, and I didn't speak.

"Did you get the book I sent?" he asked.

I hadn't. As far as I knew, he had forgotten me totally. He hadn't written, he hadn't phoned. "No," I said.

"That's Christmas mail." He smiled. "Maybe your mother will send it back down here."

"Maybe," I said.

Then Regan said something and he turned to her so quickly that you'd think he had been just passing time until he could talk to her. The intensity of his smile didn't ease off, either, when he looked at her. I got up. "I've got to check something," I said, and rushed out of the lunchroom.

It was unfair! Regan had gotten to study in New York; she got better grades in drama class than I did; in the Christmas play, she'd gotten the lead I'd wanted; and now it looked as if she was going to get, if she hadn't already gotten, Dan. I didn't want to come in second to her for the rest of my life.

When I went into drama class, I found a seat between two students who were already there. I didn't want to sit next to Dan or Regan.

Class hadn't been in session a minute before Mrs. Daly asked me to deliver an extemporaneous talk about my experiences at the audition, and I knew Regan must have told her that I'd attended one. Now the girl was telling about my life before I had a chance to do it. I was so irritated that I didn't give a thought to being afraid of being on stage without a role to play. I went through the entire thing as if I'd rehearsed, and I guess I had; I'd told the story at least three times before.

When I was finished, Mrs. Daly said I had been fortunate, but that she wasn't surprised a bit at my achievement because I had talent.

I thought if I never heard that word again it would be too soon.

After school, on the off chance Mrs. McQuaide hadn't found anyone to replace me, I went to the day-care center to see if she still wanted my help.

"Tree," she said, glad to see me, "the children will be so happy you're back."

She was right about that one. All afternoon the kids didn't want to do anything but listen to me tell them about New York City and all the things I'd done and all the things I'd seen.

"Was it cold, Treesa?"

"Did you ride a subway?"

"Treesa, tell us about the tall buildings."

"How many people were there?"

I filled them in completely, telling about the view from the top of the Empire State Building, the rides on the ferries, the dinosaur bones in the museum, the way some of the people in the Village and SoHo looked.

And it was as I talked that I had my fabulous idea.

No one, but no one, in Jacksonville had her hair cut punk. If I fixed my hair that way, Dad would know I meant business. He would see that I didn't fit here any-more and he would send me to stay with Mom at least until my hair grew out.

# Chapter Ten

On the way home from work, I stopped in a drugstore and got some wash-out colored mousse in bright red. I thought about going over to Jamie's to get her help, but I figured she would refuse; she'd think I was crazy or something. Also I considered going to a professional to get my hair cut, but I was afraid they might call my dad.

Dinner was rather strained, at least on my side, and that was because I knew what I was going to do later.

"Did your day go okay?" Dad asked.

"Yeah, sure. Fine," I said, after choking on a bite of potato.

"I wondered. It was the first day back in school after a vacation. Sometimes it's difficult to get into the swing of things again."

"No problem."

"Did you see Jamie?"

I nodded.

"Daniel?"

"He was there."

For a few minutes, we were quiet; I couldn't think about anything except what I was planning, and I sure wasn't going to tell Dad that. Usually I told him nearly every move I'd made during the day, but tonight I wasn't able to.

When he couldn't take the silence any longer, he asked, "Teresa, is anything the matter?" He paused. "I mean, anything new?"

"No," I said and looked at him. "Nothing new."

"I'm not going to change my mind."

All I did was look back down at my plate; after tonight he just might. Need I tell you nothing was said for the remainder of the meal?

I got the dishes done more quickly than I'd ever done them before, and then I went to my room.

My hair was long, below shoulder length, somewhat wavy, and a light shade of golden blond. The color ought to take well on that shade, I thought. My hair was pretty. It was one of my best features. And I'd never had any real trouble with it. But I was going to take trouble with it now.

The idea scared me.

I took a deep breath and let it out. There are some things you have to do even if they scare you.

Before I did anything else, I took a shower and washed my hair; hair was supposed to be easier to cut when it was wet. And then, with the towel wrapped around my head, I sat and thought. I wasn't sure I was brave enough to do this; everyone would look at me as if I were a freak. I knew they would because I'd done

that in New York when I'd seen strange and wild hair-
cuts and colors on the street.

But New York was where people wore their hair that
way, and that was where I was going to be.

I got up and grabbed the scissors, took off the towel
and looked at myself again.

With the scissors clutched in my right hand and a
hank of hair clutched in my left, I placed the scissors
over the hair and closed my eyes.

When I opened them, I was clutching a huge chunk
of silky blond hair. I dropped it in the wastebasket and
peered at my new image.

"Oh, no!"

I looked as if an Indian had caught me fleetingly and
had tried unsuccessfully to scalp me. One large space of
bristly scalp showed in the midst of an otherwise de-
cent-looking head of hair.

What was I going to do now?

What else could I do?

I watched as I trimmed half my hair close to the scalp;
I at least wanted it to be fairly even. But after I was finished with the left side of my head, I really did look
terrible, like someone in a carnival who was half man,
half woman.

I would have screamed but I was afraid Dad would
hear me.

My ear was so prominent. So *there*! I'd never paid
much attention to my ears—they were normal shape,
normal size, they didn't stick out and they weren't
warped, but before now they had been at least partly
covered by hair. Now my left ear wasn't obscured by
anything, and I wondered how boys could stand seeing
that odd bit of gristly flesh sticking out every day say-

ing "Look at me." But then I guessed since they'd seen such all their lives they'd gotten accustomed to the sight.

So would I. I would have to.

The right side was easier to cut. I left it about three inches long on the top and tapered it to the nape of my neck. After I finished that, I looked better. That side being shorter made the other half of my head seem less bald. I put the red mousse on and hair spray, and made the hair I had left stand up and stick out, then I turned away from the mirror to rest my eyes and the memory of how I looked.

I wanted to surprise myself with a quick look later when I wasn't expecting to see myself.

But I couldn't forget I'd practically shaved half my head. The left side of my scalp was cool and felt defenseless and vulnerable, and any time I moved, air whistled against the nearly bare skin. I would have to wear a cap if the weather was cold when I went outside; I'd never worn hats before but now I would probably freeze to death if I didn't.

For a time I worked on my school assignments, and since I wasn't moving much I forgot what I'd done until I reached up to scratch my head and felt whiskers, not hair.

I shrieked.

Not loud—it was more of a squeak and I don't think Dad could have heard me, but I clamped my hand over my mouth to keep any other noises from coming out. And then I looked at myself in the mirror.

Wow! Did I look different!

Not only did I look different from me, I looked different from everyone around here. Surely Dad would send me to where others of my kind were. This was terrific. I loved it. And it was a good thing I'd done as much of my homework as I had because I couldn't stop looking at myself. I tried to see my head from every angle; I posed and made faces and put on varied expressions until way past the time I usually went to sleep.

In the morning, I spruced up my new look and posed some more and put on my most ultra top, my peggiest pants and my ugliest shoes. But when it was time to leave my room, I lost my courage; I wasn't sure I wanted Dad to be the first person to see me like this.

It wasn't very cold out, but it was cold enough for me to get away with wearing a cap. I scrambled through my winter wear and found the biggest, floppiest one I had and fitted it down all the way to my ears. Now I looked like the old me with my hair tucked up. I stuck the mousse in my purse just in case I had to redo after I took off the cap, and I probably would, and also, thinking I might as well go all the way, I stuck in bright eye shadow and lipstick and rouge.

Dad glanced at my cap but didn't say anything about it. "Want some orange juice?" he asked.

"No, thanks, Dad. I have to leave early."

"You ought to eat something."

"I'll take an apple." As I got one from the refrigerator, the coolness penetrated the knit of my cap, and I wondered if when it really got to be cold weather I would freeze no matter what I wore. "Bye, Dad."

On the route to school, I stopped in a gas station and went into the rest room. My hair hadn't messed up much, but it had messed up some and I fixed it. And put on makeup. I looked fantastic—as in out of a fantasy.

I left the rest room and crossed toward my car, and the station attendant stopped dead what he was doing and stared at me. I gave him a smile, but he didn't move.

When I got to school I found the students clustered as usual on the steps waiting for the bell to ring. All conversation ceased as I climbed the stairs.

When I reached the top, I heard someone behind me whisper, "Tree? Is that you?"

I turned. "It's me, all right."

Bedlam broke loose. Some kids wanted to touch and some wanted to know when I'd done it, how I'd done it, why I'd done it, but some thought I was just trying to get attention and refused to give me any.

By the time everyone was through investigating, I had to go respike my hair. And when I went into home room, those who hadn't seen me on the steps froze. One of them was Jamie. She didn't freeze, she screamed.

"Shh," I said as I slipped into the seat beside her, but the teacher had heard and looked around at us and saw me and then *she* screamed.

That made everyone laugh and start to cut up and talk. It's a wonder the roll was called.

After that short period, as we were going to our first class, Jamie, mute until now, said to me, "What on earth has gotten into you? What did you do to yourself? Where is your hair?"

"It's in the wastebasket in my bedroom."

"You look like someone out of a rock group. A punk rock group. Why?"

"I figure Dad won't want me hanging around looking like this so he'll send me to Mom."

She shook her head. "You should have asked me before you did it. He'll send you to a mental institution."

"Nah."

"He will. And with cause. You're crazy!"

"I knew you'd say that."

"I say it only because it's true."

Her opinion was obviously held by others. As I had thought I would be, I was stared at, pointed at, laughed at. I didn't care. If this hair got the job on my Dad done, then I would have been successful.

Just before lunch, I saw Regan in the hall.

"Hi," I said to her.

"What happened to you?"

"Like it?" I asked, making a full turn in front of her.

"No, I don't like it."

She was the first person to have been so blunt, and she effectively stopped my modeling maneuvers.

"You've ruined yourself," she said.

"What?"

"You have gone against one of the very first principles an actor should follow."

"Oh?" I said. "And what's that?"

"To be able to fill as many roles as possible. The way you look, you could play only one type. And there aren't a lot of parts written for that type—certainly no leading parts."

That stunned me. "I hadn't thought of that."

She lifted her arms in a gesture of hopelessness. "I wish you had."

"So do I."

"Well," she said and smiled, but her smile looked forced. "You look cute, anyway."

"Thanks," I said. "A lot."

"Don't feel too bad. We'll think of something."

As if she'd been doing it since the day we met, she walked with me until we joined Jamie, and the three of us went to lunch. I knew within minutes I would see

Dan. I thought seriously about putting my cap back on, but I didn't.

"Aaa," he said when he saw me. His eyes got big and he looked shocked. "Aaaaa."

"Don't," Regan told him. "She feels bad enough."

"I don't feel bad," I said. I hadn't told her why I'd done my hair, and I wasn't about to feel bad about it. After I got to New York it would grow out and everything would be fine.

"It was you," Dan said to me.

"What was me?"

"I heard about the punker in school, and some of the kids snickered when I came around and I wondered why. Now I know why. It was you."

"I'm not an it."

"Okay, *she* was you."

"I think she looks cute," Regan said.

"Of course she looks cute."

"So?" I said. "Why'd they snicker?"

"You don't know?"

I glanced at Jamie for a clue, and she lifted her shoulders and shook her head. Regan just stared back at me. "Know what?" I asked.

Dan sagged back in his chair, seeming to be thoroughly exhausted, but I didn't know what had tired him out. "Tree," he said, "would you like to go the beach with me next Saturday if the weather's nice?"

I glanced at Regan. "I don't know," I said. "I guess so."

"Well that's a step in the right direction," he said.

"It won't embarrass you to be seen with me?"

"I think I can bear up."

He got up and started to pull my chair out for me but didn't actually do it. I thought maybe he was afraid some kids would snicker at him again, this time for being a gentleman.

"Thank you," I said.

He reached up and touched the shaved part of my head. "You look really weird, do you know that?" Then he smiled. "Cute, but weird."

The children at the day-care center were amazed at my new look, and some of them didn't recognize me. Again I didn't have to do too much work—they mainly wanted to look at me and feel my hair. Most of the girls wanted to put bright makeup like mine on, and I obliged, hoping none of the parents would object.

And then it was time to go home, and I knew this time I couldn't avoid facing Dad. But by now I was pretty much accustomed to how I felt and how people reacted to me, so I thought I could take anything he might dish out.

Especially a ticket to the city.

Still, I put my cap on before I went inside; I wanted to fix any spikes that might have fallen and add more color. I was going to do this right.

As I went past the door to the kitchen, Dad said, "Hello, Duchess," and glanced out at me. "Hey! Come back here."

My heart began to go like a marble rolling fast down stairs and, like that marble, it fell. I just knew someone had told him what I'd done. Maybe even Mrs. Mc-Quaide had phoned him.

"Yes?" I said, staying in the hallway and peeking in.

"Don't you have on too much makeup?" he asked. "I mean for street wear. Or were you in a production in drama class today?"

"No, uh—" I didn't want to *tell* him, I wanted to *show* him. "The kids at the center wanted to put make-

up on," I told him. And felt guilty even though that was
the truth; it was such a stretch of the truth that it came
close to being a lie.

"Oh," he said. "I wondered. You don't usually
wander around looking so overdone." He grinned.
"Dinner will be ready in a few minutes. I took off early
today and cooked. We're having my specialty."

Every time he cooked we had his specialty: broiled
steak and baked potato and a salad made with lettuce
and sprouts. "Great," I said. "Be back in a sec."

As I spruced up my hair and made my makeup even
more vivid, I shook from head to foot. If I'd had hair
it would have trembled. As I walked back toward the
kitchen I felt as though the floor were vibrating be-
neath my feet.

Before I went in, I cleared my throat. Whether that
was an announcement of my entrance or because of
nerves, I don't know, but Dad was looking at the door
as I came through.

His mouth dropped open and he took a step back-
ward.

I knew I wouldn't be able to talk, so I waved at him.

*"What have you done to yourself?"* he roared.

"Dad, I—"

*"What have you done?"*

"Dad," I said. "I cut my hair."

"That's not a haircut!" he yelled. "That's a mutila-
tion!"

"Lots of kids wear their hair this way in the Village."

"You don't live in the Village."

I wanted to say that I could if he would let me, but I
thought that might sound snippy, so I decided to let him
come to that decision by himself.

"You look like a...like a..." He was at a loss for words and I didn't want to help him out by supplying the word *freak*, which I was sure was what he was searching for. "Why did you do such a thing?" he ended.

"Well." I shrugged. "The kids in SoHo do their hair this way, and I liked it."

"You *like* that?"

"Sure." He wasn't taking my hint quickly enough to suit me, so I said, "I wanted to fit in."

"Like *that*?"

"In the Village. In SoHo."

He was silent a moment. I could see the light breaking in the east of his eyes.

"I want to live there, Dad."

His face started to turn red. I might have seen him angry when we landed at the airport, but now he was livid. He even shook; he trembled almost as much as I had a few minutes ago when I had been scared to face him.

But he stayed where he was, not moving, not speaking, just trembling and turning redder. I finally realized his tremors were caused by his attempt at control.

"You," he said at last, "are not going to live there."

"Dad," I said, "I've *got* to."

"You will not."

"But, Dad—"

"I cannot believe this," he said. "I cannot believe this. We have been over this same conversation a hundred times minimum and I cannot believe we're doing it again. The answer is no, Teresa. No! I don't care what pranks you pull, what you do to your appearance, you are not going to move to New York and live with your mother and that is final." He took a deep breath and said again, *"Final!"*

"Listen to me," I said. "Will you one time listen to me? Mother is there and now is the best time for me to go."

"Your mother is working at her art."

"And that's what *I* want to do. I've told you that a million times. That's what *I* want to do."

"I've heard you all those times, and I've tried to explain to you that here is where you will study for at least another year and a half."

"But Mom got to go," I wailed. "How come she gets to do it and I don't?"

I thought he might hit me. For the first time in my life I thought he was actually going to hit me. But he controlled himself again and took a few deep breaths and then said very, very patiently as if he were explaining to a feeble old person in the last stages of senility, "Your mother worked at her painting for years. She studied wherever and whenever she could. She learned everything she could learn and she practiced her craft daily. We decided long ago that when the opportunity arose, *when it arose*, then she could study elsewhere. She didn't just suddenly decide she wanted to go to New York. She *earned* the right."

He was telling me nothing I didn't know; I knew every spare moment Mom had she had spent working on her art.

"And I miss her terribly now that she's gone," he said. "I hope you never have to miss anyone the way I miss her."

The way he spoke made my heart wrench.

"She sacrificed herself," he went on. *"Sacrificed!* Do you understand the meaning of that word? I've never in my life known anyone more talented than your mother. But she sacrificed herself to help me get started in business. To give you the kind of home life she thought you deserved."

Smoke started to pour out of the oven behind him, and I knew the steaks were burning. "Dad," I said.

"And what she thinks you need now, what *I* think you need, is to do the work you can do here and earn the right to go the way she did."

"I can't stay here," I said.

"You can't go." He glared at me.

"But what about my hair?"

He glanced at my head. "*What* hair?"

"Dad," I said, "I can't live around here with my hair like this."

For a second he looked nonplussed, then he said, "You did it, Duchess. You did it to yourself."

# Chapter Eleven

Smoke had almost filled the kitchen. Dad finally noticed it and turned toward the stove. He made a noise that could have been a moan or a sob—I wasn't sure which.

"Dad?"

"I've burned dinner," he said. He went to the oven and started to take out the steaks, but he'd forgotten a pad to protect his fingers and jerked away. I could have sworn tears were in his eyes as he got a pad and tried again. I'd never seen him so distraught or inept. He almost dropped the pan as he transferred it to the sink and dumped it in.

"Dad?" I said again.

"It's okay, Duchess. It's okay," he said, but he wouldn't look at me. He kept leaning against the sink staring down at the charred mess.

"I'm sorry."

"It's not your fault."

"But—my hair."

"It isn't your fault, Teresa. It has nothing to do with your hair."

"But if I hadn't cut my hair, you wouldn't have burned the steaks."

He didn't answer and he didn't look at me. He just shook his head. He looked so sad that I was more concerned about him than I'd ever been about anybody.

"What *is* wrong, Dad?" I went to him and put my hand on his shoulder. "What *is* wrong?"

"Nothing." He said the word so softly that I almost didn't hear.

The blackened steaks lying in the sink sent tendrils of steam into the smoggy air. The kitchen smelled as if someone had doused a bonfire. Dad did nothing but stare down at the ruined steaks, but I knew he wasn't seeing them. I stared a minute, then figured someone should open some windows, and I remembered to turn off the broiler.

Dad still hadn't moved.

I felt utterly wretched. He might have said nothing was my fault, but I knew if I hadn't come into the kitchen with my hair fixed the way it was that this situation would never have come to pass: Dad would have served his dinner and everything would be as it had always been.

I turned on the fan over the stove, hoping that would help dispel the smoke.

And Dad said something.

"What?" I didn't know whether to move nearer to him or go farther away.

He cleared his throat. "I'm sorry, Duchess."

I moved nearer. "Don't be," I said. "I'm the one who should be sorry."

"It's just that—"

He broke off and I went all the way to him and put my hand on his shoulder again. "Just what, Dad?"

"Your mom."

I was instantly terrified that something had happened to her. "What about Mom?"

"She's—"

"Is she okay?" My fingers dug into him. I grabbed him and turned him to face me. "Is she okay?"

He looked at me, dazed and puzzled.

*"Is she okay?"* I all but screamed this time.

"She's fine. She's just fine." His eyes slowly brought the world back into view. "I didn't mean to startle you." He was looking at me now, not at some scene I couldn't see. "It's just that—" he straightened up, I knew it took an effort, and made his expression less disconsolate "—just that she isn't here and I miss her. That's all."

He'd scared me half to death. "That's *all*?"

His mouth twisted and I knew he was trying to smile. "Well, Duchess, for me that's enough." He turned again to the burned food and said, "I really made a botch of dinner, didn't I?"

"I'm not hungry," I said. Large in my mind loomed the way he'd said Mom being gone was enough for him, and that took away my appetite. I hadn't known he was so lonely without her.

"We could go out," he said.

"No. Really, Dad. I'm not hungry. I've got to do my homework. I'll grab a sandwich later." I stopped before I went out the door, and looked back at him. "I'm sorry I made you angry, Dad."

I didn't go to my room. I went into the living room and got the phone and took it to the farthest, most private corner, and called my mother. For a few moments after she answered, I was able to keep myself under control, and then I lost it. I sobbed out what I had done to my hair, how the kids at school had acted and how Dad had reacted and how he had burned the food and how sad he'd been. I kept my voice low so he couldn't hear me, but I didn't hold anything else back. I was so mortified that I thought I might die.

"Honey," she kept saying, "honey, don't cry."

"But, Mom, I can't stay here looking like this. I can't. I just knew he'd let me come up there if I did my hair."

"Tree, honey, we told you—"

"I *know* what you told me, but I thought—"

"Oh, honey, you knew better."

"But what am I going to do?" I wailed.

There was a short pause, then she said, "Smile."

"What?"

"Smile and make the best of it. That's all you can do. Tree, honey, I know you've got enough gumption to get through this. You've got more courage than anyone I know and if anyone can pull being drastically different off, you can. Don't let it get you down."

At the moment, those words didn't help me; I hadn't brought a handkerchief or a box of tissues and my sleeve was soaked but I didn't have anything else, so I again wiped my face on it. I felt I was maybe four years old maximum.

"Do you hear me, Tree?"

I nodded, then remembered she couldn't see me. "Yes."

"Keep your chin up."

"Okay." When I hung up, I was still leaking from my eyes and nose, so I got a tissue. And then another. Tomorrow I might not have to wear makeup; my eyes would be colorful enough.

Before I'd gotten myself together, Dad came into the room and I was glad I hadn't turned on the light.

"I'll tell you what I'll do, Duchess," he said. "This summer when you go stay with your mother, I'll pay for lessons at any drama studio in New York that will accept you."

"Oh, Dad!"

"We might as well take advantage of the fact you have a place to stay."

By then I was hugging him.

He hugged me, too, for a moment, then he held me away and tried to see me in the dim light from the hall. "Have you been crying?"

"Well, yeah, a little bit." I didn't want to tell him I'd broken down to Mom, so I said, "You know, the hair and all."

"Don't let that make you cry."

"Okay. I won't." I gave him another hug and said, "Thanks, Dad," then escaped to my bedroom.

But the next morning I felt like crying all over again. There wasn't a single thing I could do about my hair unless I bought a wig. I didn't want to admit how stupid I'd been by covering my mistake with fake hair. I had to wear it the way it was. And I had to keep coloring it and wearing wild makeup or I would look really dumb.

I sighed as I got myself together. At least I wouldn't have to make a grand entrance at school today, except maybe for Mrs. Daly. What she thought worried me more than what anyone else thought now that I knew

what Dad and Jamie and Dan thought. She might think
I was too bizarre to allow on stage even for classroom
skits.

But a substitute was teaching drama for the rest of the
week; Mrs. Daly was out with the flu.

It was fairly warm on Saturday, not warm enough to
plan on swimming because at this time of year the water was too cool, but it was warm enough so I didn't
have to bundle up for my date with Daniel. Except that
I had to wear a cap.

I was conscious of this as I climbed into Daniel's old
car. I could feel him looking at my head and I flushed.
However, he didn't say anything until we reached Beach
Boulevard, when he finally burst out with "I want to
talk to you about the way you cut your hair."

"What about it?" I asked.

"Why'd you do it?"

"I thought you knew."

"I don't."

"I thought the reason would be obvious to anyone
who knew me. I figured looking like this would convince Dad to send me to New York."

"You did that to yourself because you thought—"
He cut off abruptly and for three miles at least he was
silent. Then he said, "You want to go to New York *that*
much?"

"You said I looked cute. Didn't you mean it?"

"Of course I meant what I said. You'd look cute
completely bald, but that's because—" He blushed. "I
don't know why you want to get away from here so
fast," he said crossly. "I can tell you the idea doesn't do
much for the male ego."

"Male ego?"

"And you got so uppity last fall you scarcely spoke to me. I can tell you I was never so surprised in my life to get a gift from you at Christmas."

"*I* got uppity with *you*?"

"Yes, you got uppity with me. After you didn't get the lead in the play, you changed. You got so snobbish you scarcely gave anyone the time of day, much less me. You avoided me."

I couldn't believe what I was hearing; it hadn't been me who had avoided him but the other way around. "I did not."

"You were a bad sport about losing the part."

"I was not."

"And you went on and on and *on* about New York as if you couldn't wait to get away from here and everyone who lived here. That wasn't very flattering."

"You knew why I wanted to go," I said. "And it wasn't me who avoided you. You quit your after-school job so you could be with Regan."

"You never gave a thought to anyone else! You didn't care how anyone else felt!" He was getting madder and madder by the minute, and I noticed that he was increasing his speed.

"You'd better slow down."

He did, and got in the right-hand lane, then gave me a chastening look. "You got so self-centered I didn't think I knew you anymore."

"You didn't *try* to know me anymore!"

"And the first thing you did after you came back home after Christmas was to cut your hair in the weirdest way imaginable because you thought you would get to go back to New York if you did."

"I don't want to talk about my hair!" I shrieked. "I won't talk about my hair. If you want to fight, I'll fight, but it won't be about my hair, it'll be about how you dropped me. Flat dropped me when you got so stuck up about getting the part of the Nutcracker."

"I didn't drop you."

"You couldn't wait to get to practice with Regan. You were all agog to get to practice with Regan. You hid in dark corners to practice with Regan."

He pulled over and stopped the car and looked at me. "I did not."

"You were seen," I said very haughtily. "But maybe you two weren't practicing. I can't think of one scene from that play that anyone would practice in a corner." Now *I* was getting madder by the minute. "And that's just what you were seen doing. Take me home."

"What?"

"I said, take me home."

He sounded amazed. "We're almost at the beach."

"I don't care. Take me home."

"All right," he said, already turning around, "if that's the way you're going to be, then I will."

We drove home in a cold silence. When we reached my driveway, he slammed on the brakes. "I just may start dating Regan," he said as I reached for the door handle.

I jumped out of the car and ran into the house as fast as I could go and ran right into Mom.

"Mom," I said, "what are you doing here?"

She smiled and touched my short-short hair. "You really did do it, didn't you?"

"That's not all I did," I said. "I just made Daniel so mad he'll never speak to me again." I burst into tears. She was going to think I'd turned into a faucet.

We stumbled to the sofa and sat down and I sobbed against her and told her how Daniel had accused me and how I had accused him and she sympathized, but then I saw her stuff all around and got enough of a handle on myself to ask again what she was doing here.

She didn't answer for a moment or two. She got up and paced around the various articles and sort of twisted one hand with the other, then she stopped and looked at me. "I've decided to move back home. I've done about all I can do toward making contacts and studying, and you were right when you said I could send my work from here, so I've come home."

"To stay?"

"Yes. I don't think I realized how difficult things were for your father until you called the other night. That set me thinking."

"To stay?" I said again, knowing what that meant; no matter what Dad had promised about the lessons this summer I wouldn't be able to take them if I had nowhere to live.

Just then, Dad slammed into the house. The door banged against the wall and knocked a picture loose. He was absolutely beaming; I'd never seen him look so happy. He and Mom flew at each other and hugged as if they hadn't seen each other in a decade instead of just a little over a week, and both of them started talking at once. They were so full of joy that I felt like a creep for thinking about my lost chance.

Why had she come back so soon? Why hadn't she stayed just a few more months?

Now I knew any hope of going to New York before I turned eighteen was totally, totally gone.

I didn't want them to see I wasn't as jubilant as they were, so I did my vanishing act. And, inconsiderate as this may sound, it took me the rest of the weekend to get over feeling sorry for myself and get into being glad to have a mom around again. And I must admit it was Dad's ultimate delight that got me adjusted that quickly.

At school the next day, Regan joined me in the corridor on the way to lunch. We caught up with Jamie, who was heading in the same direction.

I wanted to tell her about Mom being home, but I didn't until we'd found a table. To my credit, I was able to put enthusiasm in the news, but Jamie, for a brief moment, in empathy, looked as disappointed as I had felt at the first.

Regan, having not had to go through the many traumas I'd been through in my attempts to get to go to New York, simply said, "I think that's great."

Dan not showing up for lunch with us wasn't great. As far as I knew, he didn't even come to the lunchroom.

He was in drama class, and he looked at me when I came in. An empty seat was beside him, but I didn't know whether to sit there or not. He didn't say anything to me, and he made no indication that he wanted me to sit by him; however, he didn't say anything to Regan, either. I couldn't make up my mind what to do. As it turned out, I didn't have to.

Mrs. Daly was back.

"Teresa Carson!" she said loudly and appalled, and then she made a sound of unfeigned horror.

Everyone in class looked at her, then at me, then at her again as if we were playing tennis.

"Come here," she ordered.

I moved toward her on feet that acted as though I was wearing ten-pound shoes.

The moment I got close enough, she took me by the shoulders and turned me around and inspected my head. "Well, that tears it," she said. "You were scheduled to play the lead in our next production, but you certainly can't do it looking like that."

I stared at her for one agonized moment, then I turned and fled. I didn't care if I got suspended or expelled for cutting class, I simply could not stay.

When I reached the girls' room, I pushed in and ran to the far corner and leaned against the wall. I didn't cry. I was too destroyed to cry.

Everything in my life had gone wrong. As badly as I had wanted to go to New York before I graduated and as hard as I'd tried, I hadn't been able to go. Now I wouldn't get to go even for the summer. Daniel thought I was a self-centered snob and I had probably lost his friendship forever. And now, because I had punked my hair in an attempt to force Dad to let me go to New York to be in the theater, I couldn't be in plays here.

I'd ruined my life.

# Chapter Twelve

I hadn't been in the rest room long before Regan came in. "I thought this was where you'd be," she said.

She looked so normal and so pretty with her simply cut hair and traditional pants and top that I felt even worse. "You'd better go back to class," I said.

"Maybe I'd better, but I'm not going to."

"You'll get kicked out of school."

"No I won't." She came to lean against the wall beside me. "And even if I do, I don't care. Friends are more important than school."

She'd never called me a friend before. It sounded good. "I don't want you to get into trouble."

"You're the one who's in trouble, or you think you are, and I thought you needed some help."

"Who can help *me*? I've wrecked everything."

"No you haven't. You cut your hair, that's all."

I snorted. "That's enough."

"It's nothing. There *are* wigs, you know."

"Yeah, but I don't have one. And even if I did I don't know if I'd wear it. Not now. Not after everyone has seen me. They'd think I was ashamed of myself."

She smiled, a tiny touch of a smile. "And you're not?"

In answer to that, I tucked my shirt in more neatly at my waist and tried to ignore her.

"Why'd you do it?" she asked.

Again I had to explain my motivation.

"You ought to be glad your father didn't send you off to New York," she said. "You wouldn't like it there."

"I love it."

"I mean, you wouldn't like studying drama. I know. I did it. And I've already had more opportunities here to exercise my craft than I did in two years there. So many people live in the city and in places nearby, and then there are those like you wanted to be. They come from all over. And the classes, if you can get in one, are so crowded with talented people you rarely get a chance to perform. Do you think I would have gotten to play Clara if I hadn't been here? No way. Too many others up there have had more training and more experience, and they would have shoved me under the table. Where do you think they get that training and experience? Somewhere else mostly, like here, like in school, unless they are prodigies or are rich. It costs a lot to live there and study privately. You need to learn as much as you can and go as far as you can before you invest in that."

"But you learned."

"Sure I did. Of course I did. You can learn by watching television, too, but that doesn't give you much time on stage, does it?"

That made me smile. "I guess not."

"So don't feel bad that you didn't get to go."

"Well. I don't feel *as* bad."

"Then I'm glad you came to the girls' room and I got to talk to you. Daniel was looking for you. He wanted to talk to you too."

I blinked. "He wanted to talk to me?"

"Are you kidding? He was out of the classroom before I was."

The last time I'd seen him he had been angry with me and threatening to date her. "Dan was?"

"He was in a real fret about you. I've never seen him so concerned. He almost came in here with me."

"He did?" The thought of him being worried about me enough to come in the girls' rest room made me feel a little bit better, but I still was unsure about how he felt about Regan. "Where is he now?"

"I suppose he went back to class. I told him if I didn't come right out that meant I'd found you."

I smiled. "At least *he* won't get kicked out of school for playing hooky."

"No one will."

Now that the subject of Dan had been broached, I wasn't about to let it go until I found out how he felt about her and she felt about him. But I had to delay to give myself time to get my courage up, so I went to the mirror and looked at myself. I did look peculiar. I tweaked at the longer half of my hair and said as casually as I could, "Did you and Dan date much while you were rehearsing the Christmas play?"

"Date?"

"Yeah. Date."

"Daniel and me?"

"Yeah."

She went into gales of laughter.

"What's so funny?" I asked.

"You," she said, trying not very successfully to stifle her fit. "I'll tell you, you're lucky I'm speaking to you. While Daniel and I worked on that play he talked about you so much I thought I never wanted to see you or hear your name again." She wiped her eyes. "No. We didn't date. He even quit his job so we could practice in the afternoon. I think he was afraid to see me at night for fear you'd be jealous. I had to practically tackle him in hallways and stuff so we could get enough rehearsals in."

"Regan," I said, feeling happier than I had in what seemed like centuries, "you're a good friend."

That stopped her laughing. Momentarily. "Well, of course I am. What else?" She giggled again. "Come on, we'd better get back to class."

"I don't want to go!" I said. "I don't ever want to go again!"

"Why not?"

"Mrs. Daly is mad at me. She said I'd blown my chance for the lead in the spring play."

"Aah, don't worry about that. There are wigs and ways around a cropped head. We'll think of something." She took me by the arm and led me out the door.

Daniel hadn't gone back to class; he was standing across the corridor from the rest-room door, waiting.

The instant Regan saw him, she said, "See you guys later," and headed for class.

Dan and I just stood there and looked at each other for a minute or two. Then he came hesitantly toward me. "Terry," he said, "I'm sorry."

"I'm the one who should apologize," I said.

"No. You didn't know how I felt. How could you? I never told you. Don't you know the reason I took drama class was to be near you?"

My ears couldn't believe what they were hearing, and my eyes couldn't believe how somber he looked. "But I . . . I thought—"

"I'm also sorry you can't have the lead in the spring play," he said.

"It's my fault. I shouldn't have cut my hair."

"But I know you feel bad about it."

"I do." This was a less volatile subject and I certainly wasn't embarrassed to talk about losing a role; it seemed as if half my conversations revolved around that subject. "But the really horrible part about it is, that lady at the auditions in New York told me I should land roles. She said what I needed most was experience on stage, and I know she was giving me good advice."

"I'm sure she was. The best way to learn something is to do it."

I laughed a little. "Yeah, I know. I've said that to myself, and I've also asked myself how can I get experience if no one will let me on a stage."

"You've got a point there."

"I can't keep writing little plays for kids. I've got to have something meaty. I've got to have a lead in a major production."

"Well, maybe next year you'll be able to land one. Your hair will have grown out by then."

"I can't wait. I want a lead this year. And one way or another, I'm going to get it. What we have to do is think up a play I *can* do," I said, "and convince Mrs. Daly to direct it."

"She does classics in the spring," he said with a worried expression. "What classic is there that needs a half-bald female lead?"

"I'm not half-bald," I said. "Granted, half my hair is very, very short, but I'm not bald."

"All right, then," he said with a grin, "what play requires a girl with very, very short hair on one side?"

"One of Shakespeare's," I said with a snap of my fingers. "Not with short hair on one side, but with short hair on both sides. And if I cut one side I can surely cut the other."

He chuckled. "I won't argue with that."

"And then I'll look like a boy."

"Well, I wouldn't go so far as to say that," he said, "but on stage it might work."

"And somewhere there's a Shakespearean play where a girl disguises herself as a boy."

"What play is it?"

"I don't remember." I grabbed his hand and dragged him along behind me. "Come with me to the library and we'll look for it. I know I'll recognize it if I see it."

I got a copy of *The Complete Works of William Shakespeare* and he took another. "Just look at the cast of characters," I told him. "The character will have a double name."

Within a minute I found what I thought was the right play. *Twelfth Night*. I scanned a bit of it. Viola pretended to be Cesario. "I've got it," I said too loudly, and the librarian shushed me. I moved closer to Dan. "This is it," I whispered.

"Are you sure?"

"I'm sure. Let's check the book out."

As we left the library with the book in hand, Daniel said, "Did it ever occur to you that Mrs. Daly might not speak to us? She might be mad at us because we've cut more than half her class."

"She'll talk," I said. "I'll make her listen."

Dan chuckled. "I believe you will."

Instead of being angry, Mrs. Daly was apologetic. "Tree," she said after we appeared suddenly beside where she sat in the audience watching pantomimes on stage. She put her hand over mine. "I'm sorry. I didn't mean to humiliate you in front of the class."

"That's okay," I said. "You hadn't seen me, and I know I look different."

She smiled. "To put it mildly."

"But you made me think about looking the way I do, and I came up with an idea," I said.

She didn't hear me because at the same time she was saying, "There's no reason why you couldn't wear a wig and play the part I had in mind for you."

"But I have had an absolute brainstorm," I said. "Look." I handed her the book opened to *Twelfth Night*. "Have you ever done this play? If you want to, now would be a better time than any other. I could be Viola." I laughed and flipped my short hair. "If I take off the other side of my hair, I certainly would look right to play that role, and instead of a girl having to stuff long hair up into a boy's wig to look like Cesario, I could wear a wig when I played Viola."

"You know something, Tree? I think you're right." She thumbed through a few pages, then looked at me. "I'm sure this would be a wonderful play to do this spring."

I almost exploded with joy. "We can do it?"

"I don't know why not."

"And I can be Viola?"

She grinned. "Who else?"

It was all I could do to keep from whooping in delight, but I contained myself and said, "Will Regan be in the play? I want to work with her again. I don't think I appreciated it as much as I should have the first time we worked together."

"I'm sure she will," Mrs. Daly said.

"And I'm sure we'll find a part for your boyfriend, too," Mrs. Daly said.

That made me blush. I practically shoved Dan out of the row of seats so I wouldn't have to answer her.

Dan laughed half under his breath as we headed for the back of the room. "Dan," I said, "about wanting to go to New York..."

"I understand," he said. "And I think it's a great idea. For the future."

For the first time, I realized having to stay here hadn't ruined my life; it had made it better. "But, Dan," I said, "when I do go, I'm going to miss you."

"Will you?" he asked. "I knew you'd come to your senses. But don't worry too much about it. Next year I'm going to junior college here, and the year after that I'll transfer to a university up north."

"You'll be near me?"

"You'd better believe it," he said.

| QUANTITY | BOOK # | ISBN # | TITLE | AUTHOR | PRICE |
|---|---|---|---|---|---|
| ☐ | 129 | 06129-3 | The Ghost of Gamma Rho | Elaine Harper | $1.95 |
| ☐ | 130 | 06130-7 | Nightshade | Jesse Osborne | 1.95 |
| ☐ | 131 | 06131-5 | Waiting for Amanda | Cheryl Zach | 1.95 |
| ☐ | 132 | 06132-3 | The Candy Papers | Helen Cavanagh | 1.95 |
| ☐ | 133 | 06133-1 | Manhattan Melody | Marilyn Youngblood | 1.95 |
| ☐ | 134 | 06134-X | Killebrew's Daughter | Janice Harrell | 1.95 |
| ☐ | 135 | 06135-8 | Bid for Romance | Dorothy Francis | 1.95 |
| ☐ | 136 | 06136-6 | The Shadow Knows | Becky Stewart | 1.95 |
| ☐ | 137 | 06137-4 | Lover's Lake | Elaine Harper | 1.95 |
| ☐ | 138 | 06138-2 | In the Money | Beverly Sommers | 1.95 |
| ☐ | 139 | 06139-0 | Breaking Away | Josephine Wunsch | 1.95 |
| ☐ | 140 | 06140-4 | What I Know About Boys | McClure Jones | 1.95 |
| ☐ | 141 | 06141-2 | I Love You More Than Chocolate | Frances Hurley Grimes | 1.95 |
| ☐ | 142 | 06142-0 | The Wilder Special | Rose Bayner | 1.95 |
| ☐ | 143 | 06143-9 | Hungarian Rhapsody | Marilyn Youngblood | 1.95 |
| ☐ | 144 | 06144-7 | Country Boy | Joyce McGill | 1.95 |
| ☐ | 145 | 06145-5 | Janine | Elaine Harper | 1.95 |
| ☐ | 146 | 06146-3 | Call Back Yesterday | Doreen Owens Malek | 1.95 |
| ☐ | 147 | 06147-1 | Why Me? | Beverly Sommers | 1.95 |
| ☐ | 149 | 06149-8 | Off the Hook | Rose Bayner | 1.95 |
| ☐ | 150 | 06150-1 | The Heartbreak of Haltom High | Dawn Kingsbury | 1.95 |
| ☐ | 151 | 06151-X | Against the Odds | Andrea Marshall | 1.95 |
| ☐ | 152 | 06152-8 | On the Road Again | Miriam Morton | 1.95 |
| ☐ | 159 | 06159-5 | Sugar 'n' Spice | Janice Harrell | 1.95 |
| ☐ | 160 | 06160-9 | The Other Langley Girl | Joyce McGill | 1.95 |

Your Order Total                                      $ _____

☐ (Minimum 2 Book Order)
New York and Arizona residents
add appropriate sales tax                             $ _____

Postage and Handling                                      .75

I enclose                                              _____


Name_____

Address_____

City_____

State/Prov._____Zip/Postal Code_____

FL-RO-2

# WATCH FOR THESE TITLES FROM FIRST LOVE COMING NEXT MONTH

---

### RACHEL'S RESISTANCE
### Nicole Hart
*A Hart Mystery*

While vacationing in France, Rachel and her friends stumbled on a secret that not only endangered their lives but threatened her brand-new French boyfriend.

### A DASH OF PEPPER
### Katrina West

Could art and science ever get together? Ask Pepper, who made a surprising discovery when she became friends with Logan Mitchells.

### PARROTS AND MONKEYS
### Beverly Sommers

Jenny was furious when her mother, a travel writer, dragged her off to the jungles of Peru. We should all be so lucky.

### ASK ME NO QUESTIONS
### Lisa Swazey

Though all the guys were after her, Logan refused to date. Why? Kirk was determined to find out.

*First Love from Silhouette*

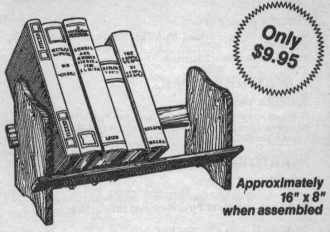